BEWARE OF GREEKS
A *Trojan Murders* Mystery

Peter Tonkin

First published in 2020 by Sharpe Books

For:
Cham, Guy, Mark and Lana as always.

CONTENTS

‘Then Helen, offspring of Zeus, answered him, “This is the son of Laertes, resourceful Odysseus, who was bred in the land of Ithaca, rugged country though it is, and is master of all kinds of trickery and clever plans.”’

Homer *The Iliad* tr Martin Hammond

1 - Captain Odysseus

i

I was born in Aulis, seaport to the great city of Thebes, youngest son to a family of merchants. Indulged by my elders without exception or limit, I grew into a capricious and demanding youth who insisted on going everywhere and seeing everything our traders had to show me. By the time I approached manhood, therefore, I had voyaged to the most distant outposts of our trading empire which reached as far to the east as the slave markets of Miletus and Phoenician Tyre, and even farther to the west: beyond the Berber Sea and as far as the Gates of Gades which some call the Pillars of Hercules.

My favourite of the many ports and cities I visited was Troy. I returned to Troy as often as I could and grew to know every street and alley from the docks to the royal palace; from the teeming wharves to the walls of the citadel which were still being repaired after a massive quaking of the earth—the work of the god Poseidon, according to local legend. Strong though they had been, they were further damaged during a pirate raid by several famous heroes led by Hercules, which had resulted in the death of King Laomedon and the succession of his son King Priam more than two generations earlier.

In those days, Troy was a rich and important city, famous as an entrepot for a range of goods from well-bred horses to jewels, scents, exotic fabrics and spices – and, most importantly, metals. It was the centre for much of the trade in copper and tin from which our metalsmiths made bronze. The cunning Trojan traders and their Greek counterparts like my father, changed copper and tin not only into bronze—but into gold; which they kept locked in their coffers or invested in ever-richer enterprises. As the murderous attack by Hercules and his pirates proved, however, Troy was a tempting target for men whose designs were less than honest, despite the height of its walls and the massive size of its gates.

In fact the place had three names, which reflected the various peoples which packed its teeming streets, temples and squares. To the local Mysian Anatolians who ruled the thin coastal strip on which the city stood, it was Ilium. To the Hittites whose great empire stretched away to the east, but pressed ever westward, threatening to squeeze the last Anatolians into the Aegean Sea, it was Wilusa. And to us Greeks—many of whom called ourselves Achaeans in those days—it was Troy. Whatever its name, it was a place of almost magical attraction, of mystery and fascination. Sometimes it seemed like an outpost of Achaean influence with so many Greeks bustling there. But it also heaved with the Anatolians, their language as strange as their clothing and their accents—even when they attempted Greek—impenetrable. But it seemed like an outpost of the Hittite empire as well, with its veiled women, its strange rites and practices which had begun to spread ever further westward, into some of the islands in the middle of the Aegean. Exotic beliefs made more alien still through the influences of the Phoenician, Egyptian and Assyrian traders who came and went amongst all the others.

But for the most part, those rulers who answered to High King Agamemnon in Mycenae kept to ancient Achaean traditions. At that time our king Thersander in Thebes, followed the western practice of having only one wife. Even Agamemnon only had one wife, the beautiful Clytemnestra. King Priam, on the other hand, ruled over a harem in the eastern fashion. Queen Hecuba was only the senior of his spouses and, below his official wives, he had numerous concubines. Agamemnon had four children but only one son—Orestes. Priam had at least fifty—the eldest was Hector and the youngest was Paris. In a city with such a ruler, there was an air of license. Anything was possible. Anything could be purchased if the price was right; anything at all. It was like a cesspool into which the dregs of the Aegean drained. Such men naturally tended to congregate in the less wholesome areas of the lower city and the docks.

And it was several such men who set upon me, cudgelled me to the ground, robbed me, and left me for dead one night as I was returning from the upper city to my ship.

Saved from death and carried aboard by my captain, I awoke at home in Aulis to find that my life had changed. My broken leg healed as well as could be expected but I limped now and could neither run nor climb. My left arm had not fared so well.

It was little more than a club, capable of holding firmly but with limited movement except in my hand which could still close to a fist. Most disastrously of all, the damage to my face and head had affected my eyes and my vision was restricted. I could still see, but not well and with occasional flashes—as though a thunderstorm in my head was throwing great bolts of lightning across what little I could perceive. In short, I was no longer any use whatsoever upon a trading vessel and a considerable liability into the bargain. The physicians to whom my grieving parents took me explained that my condition was unlikely to improve—indeed, my sight might deteriorate.

Determined not to become a helpless burden, I demanded that my father find me some occupation I could follow, even in my current condition. He sent me to his partner in the city of Chalcis, Aulis' sister port which stood on the Island of Euboea a couple of leagues distant across a narrow strait. Father's partner put me to work in his warehouses. Here I was tutored by his Cretan record keeper in the art of making marks upon clay tablets. I reluctantly learned to incise the simple characters that recorded what goods went in and out and made a manifest of what remained. The Cretan told me of others trained like him who worked at the major trading houses and even at the court of the High King where the strange symbols could record messages passed from one great monarch to another. The Hittites also had such a system, but the Achaean system and the Hittite one did not match. Such things were unknown amongst the lesser kings in any case, he said, but if I applied myself he could teach me much about this strange process that he called writing. However, I found the work impossibly boring and soon returned home, feeling bitterly helpless and useless.

***

But as the Fates would have it, as I made my halting way across Aulis' busy agora one afternoon soon after my return from Chalcis, I came across Stasinus the rhapsode. He was seated in a space among the market stalls, at the centre of an admiring crowd who were demonstrating their appreciation of his work by placing money, food and drink in front of him. What I could see of the man was not impressive despite his expensive clothing. He was old, hunched, and thin as a twig. One of his legs was twisted and a crutch lay by his side. I got close enough to perceive that one of his eyes was milk-white and the other had an unsettling squint. However, his importance lay not in what he looked like but in what he sounded like. In a voice as clear and resonant as that of the famous rhapsode Orpheus himself, he was reciting a lyric telling of nymphs and shepherds on the slopes of Mount Olympus. His words seemed to have a strange power as he told of the puny mortals and the eternal gods and goddesses watching them at play. I found I was entranced and full of an excitement I could hardly find words to express.

When Stasinus was finished and the crowd was gone, I helped him collect his payment and began the task of talking him into accepting me as his apprentice as I guided him towards a nearby tavern. I had, I maintained, many of the qualifications to be a rhapsode already. I had an excellent memory, which could be further sharpened with practise. I had an arm suited for holding a lyre—if for little else. I limped, though I was not precisely crippled. Most persuasive of all, I was partially sighted, like Stasinus himself, a fact which promised to sharpen my memory even further, the loss of one sense seemingly balanced by the acquisition of other strengths. It took some time to win him over, but my family was wealthy and supportive after the disaster of my employment in the warehouse, and in the face of my sudden overpowering enthusiasm. Some gold changed hands and there was the promise of a new lyre, which eventually overcame any reservations Stasinus might have had.

As the seasons passed, while my vision settled and my leg strengthened, Stasinus taught me the basic chords I needed to enliven the pastoral lyrics he made me commit, word for word, into my memory. But only one of his songs really interested me—an epic that he in turn had learned at the knee of his own master. This told the tale of Captain Jason, his famous crew, the good ship *Argo* and their voyage to Colchis. In fact, it was a voyage that I had made myself in these more modern times, following the route that Captain Jason had explored, so I began to add details from my own experience. It was also a voyage that Hercules had undertaken as one of the *Argo*'s crew before he jumped ship with his companion Hylas and went pirating to Troy instead. As I added detail after detail—much to Stasinus' disapproval—I began to wonder what an epic that told of Hercules' raid on Troy might sound like. Something deep within me, it seemed, blamed the city I had once loved for the injuries done to me on the docks there, so planning a song about its destruction seemed to satisfy some profound if unexpected need in me. In my imagination I began to follow Hercules from his ship to the gate of the lower town, up the hill and through the Scaean Gates into the Citadel, then into the Royal Palace itself in the days when old King Priam was younger even than young Prince Paris was now.

In the face of my master's disapproval, I spent more time down on the dockside where my father's ships were moored, and in the taverns frequented by his men—who knew me and would watch out for me should anyone try to take advantage of my situation. It was in one of these taverns that my life changed once again.

I was seated by the fire, lyre in hand, eyes closed as I struck the strings and sang. I had just finished one of my master's pastoral lyrics and was beginning a new epic of my own, following Hercules in my memory and with my words on his fatal path toward the Citadel, the Palace and the doomed King Laomedon. '*Sing, Muses, of the anger of Hercules, black and murderous, costing the Trojans terrible sorrow, casting King Laomedon into Hades' dark realm leaving his royal corpse for the dogs and the ravens. Begin with the bargain between the old king and Godlike Hercules. Strong promises the old king broke calling forth the rage of the son of Zeus…*'

My song followed Hercules as he prowled through the streets I knew so well, through the lower gates in the outer wall, through the lower city, past the vacant night-time agora with its empty market stalls, up towards the citadel and the palace and the king.

Until a quiet voice commanded, 'Stop.'

ii

I obeyed, falling silent and opening my eyes to find myself confronted by a man perhaps ten years my senior; a well-built, solid man of middle height whose red curls and short, thick beard seemed to gleam with bronze in the firelight. The fire also revealed a pair of deep-set eyes that were the blue of the sea at the furthest horizon on a calm summer's afternoon. He wore a cloak and beneath it a richly figured tunic which ended just above his knees. In doing so it revealed a scar which ran up the outside of his left thigh, a pale ridge along the bronzed flesh of his leg. He presented no threat and my father's crewmen sat well back, observing him with awe.

'You seem to know Troy well,' he said. 'Unless you learned the song from some other rhapsode.' His voice was deep, his tone abrupt – that of someone used to unquestioning obedience.

'The song is mine. I know the place,' I said.

'I might be able to use a man who knows Troy as well as you seem to,' he said.

'Even a man who is half blind?' I asked. My dull gaze met his dazzling one and he nodded as he assessed the damage to my face and my eyes.

'Even a man who, sitting in a tavern in Aulis, nevertheless can guide me through the back streets and dark alleys of Troy up to the palace of Priam himself,' he said at last.

'Are you Hercules reborn then?' I asked. 'Planning to pirate the place?'

'No, lad. I am Captain Odysseus and I mean what I say.'

'Odysseus,' I said. 'You share that name with the King of Ithaca. As you share that scar on your left thigh.'

'As I have been told,' said Captain Odysseus, 'many times before.'

'The King of Ithaca,' my father mused when I told him of my new acquaintance later that evening. 'A man whose cleverness borders on cunning, not to say deviousness by all accounts. What does such a man want with you?'

'He wants someone to sing to his crewmen aboard his ship *Thalassa*, he says,' I answered. 'Lyrics Stasinus taught me of the mountains and fields would be as acceptable as epics of the sea and pirates such as Jason son of Aeson and Hercules who called himself son of Zeus.'

'Someone who knows the back-streets of Troy like the back of his hand, more like,' mused my father. 'Someone who could go in there unnoticed and come out again unremarked. Because who would take any notice of a half-blind rhapsode limping here and there and singing the odd song?' he paused. 'Who but Odysseus would see the potential you could represent?'

'Troy?' I asked, bemused, failing to remark that Father, also noted for his deviousness, had seen the potential for spying I seemed to represent as clearly as the cunning King of Ithaca. 'What about Troy?'

'It's all over the docks,' he explained. 'It has been for some time, though it may have escaped the attention of you and your rhapsodic master. King Agamemnon's planning a raid.'

'Against Troy?' I said. 'Why?'

'He says it's to retrieve his brother's wife Helen, stolen away by Prince Paris. But it's more likely to extend his own power eastwards onto both shores of the Aegean. Not to mention adding enormously to his already considerable wealth and reputation, as Hercules did all those years ago before I was even born. If he uses Troy as a focal point, he might even manage to sweep the Anatolians off the Aegean's eastern shore altogether. Put himself hard up against the Hittites. Stop them coming westward—unless they make him an offer he finds irresistible. He's apparently planning to assemble an enormous army and expects to win a great victory in a matter of months.'

'Months?' I said, remembering Troy's stout outer walls and that massive central citadel whose fortifications were made of huge stone blocks which sloped upwards and inwards. They were more than a kalamos, 15 feet, wide at the base and much more than that to the top. Even Hercules could not have got over them had not Poseidon broken them first. 'It'll take *years* more likely!' I scoffed.

And, as I had failed to remark my father's cunning, I failed to hear the Fates laughing.

***

'Your crafty new friend appears to agree with you,' nodded Father. 'I hear he pretended to be mad rather than obey High

King Agamemnon of Mycenae's call to arms because he feared such a lengthy campaign. Either that or he's a coward.'

'He's no coward,' I said. 'And he seems fully committed to Agamemnon now.'

'Because he has no choice. Ithaca cannot afford to have Mycenae as an enemy and the High King is not a forgiving man. So Odysseus is on a recruiting drive,' said Father. 'Not after soldiers I'll wager. He'll be after kings and princes—generals who come with armies ready-made. And I can see his reasoning: the more great commanders he can persuade to join the High King, the shorter the war will be. Did he say where he's bound?'

'North to Phthia,' I said.

'Phthia and King Peleus,' he said, hooding his eyes, as he tended to do when his own slyness came close to rivalling Odysseus' famous cunning.

'But I thought King Peleus was old,' I said. 'One of the few remaining of the same generation as Hercules and Jason. Completely under the thumb of his wife Queen Thetis.'

'He's not after poor old Peleus,' said Father in the tone he reserved for instructing backward children. 'He's after the old man's only son Prince Achilles. Achilles and his army of Myrmidons.'

'But there are hundreds of Myrmidons,' I gasped. 'That's why they're named for ants—that and their black armour.'

'Precisely. And they'll be just one element of the army Agamemnon is planning to build. It will be huge. And it will all be camped on a barren beach at the edge of the great plain beneath the city called the Troad. To begin with, at any rate. They'll set up within striking distance of Troy and take it from there. That's a seven-day voyage from here, depending on wind and tide.' A look of calculation entered his eyes. 'And if you and your friend Odysseus are right, Agamemnon will soon find he has an enormous army stuck on a beach in front of an invulnerable city, locked in a lengthy siege—and crying out for supplies. Especially if the Trojans clear the Troad of everything to eat or drink and the other nearby cities of Lyrnessus, Lukka and Miletus prove unwilling to provide provisions and are hard to sack in turn.' He pulled at his beard, as he always did while completing some delicate calculation or hatching some devious scheme. Then he continued. 'And what if the youngest son of a major trading house had the ear of a senior general in the matter of supplies, deadlines and prices? A trading house ready, willing and able to supply anything from spears to sheep, wine to war chariots…' His eyes shone at the prospect. Wars were a source of immeasurable profit to trading houses such as ours, especially long wars. 'Pack what you need,' he said. 'Your brothers will help you get down to the docks before Captain Odysseus gets impatient and decides to go without you. And don't forget to kiss your mother goodbye before you go. You may not be back for some time.'

iii

'No,' said Odysseus as we prepared to set sail next day aboard his ship, which he had named *Thalassa* in the same manner as Jason had named his vessel *Argo*. 'When I am in my palace in Ithaca, you may call me "King". When I am in my war chariot on the battlefield, then you may call me "General". But here…' he stamped his foot on the boards decking the rear of his ship, 'here aboard *Thalassa* you call me "Captain".'

And I, so pleased and excited to be aboard at his side, was happy to do so. Even though I did not yet fully understand what it was he saw in me or what he had planned for me, in spite of my father's suspicions.

'Ah,' he continued as his gaze moved down to the dockside to watch the last few men preparing to come aboard. 'You may find you have some problems with your songs about Jason and Hercules in the immediate future, boy.'

'How so, Captain?' I asked.

'You see that old man down there?' he pointed to the forward gangplank at the far end of the ship.

I strained my eyes to focus. Beyond the occasional flash of brightness at the edge of my vision, I could just make out the man the Captain was talking about. His thin white hair and thick white beard belied the upright figure, energetic movement and soldier's commanding bearing.

'That's Nestor of Geronia, King of Pylos. High King

Agamemnon's chief advisor, wished on me for the duration of this mission. I don't think Agamemnon really trusts me yet.' He dropped his voice to little more than a whisper. 'And, as you'll soon find out, I'm not the only one with a problem.'

I looked at him in surprise, eyebrows raised in mute enquiry.

'*Your* problem is that King Nestor is among the last of a dying breed. As a young man he was one of Jason's crew aboard the *Argo*. He knew Hercules, though he did not take part in his raid on Troy. But that won't stop him telling you all about both Jason and Hercules at almost inexhaustible length.' He paused, thought for a moment then continued, still in little more than a whisper. '*My* problem is that the High King thinks he's a truly great advisor but for all the wrong reasons. He's a good speaker, easy to listen to, persuasive. He's widely experienced—knew all the great men of the earlier generations as I say; those who were adventuring before *I* was born, let alone *you*. He sailed with them, fought alongside them; outlived them for the most part. No matter what the problem he's asked to advise on, he's been in a position just like it which he's happy to describe at great length. Then his advice is a mixture of how he and his companions handled the situation at that time, regardless of the actual outcome. That, and what he thinks the High King wants to hear.'

'But surely,' I said, 'those are the very things by which a great advisor should be measured.'

'No, lad,' he said as King Nestor leaped aboard and waved towards the Captain along the length of the vessel. 'The worth of an advisor should be measured by the results of his advice.'

The elderly king came bounding up the deck. 'My people are all aboard,' he announced as he arrived beside us. 'Cast off whenever you like. Who's this?'

'Ship's rhapsode,' answered Captain Odysseus easily. 'I brought him aboard to entertain the crew.'

'Oh,' said Nestor. Then, hardly pausing for breath he continued, 'of course on the *Argo* Captain Jason recruited Orpheus to entertain us as we voyaged to Colchis. Not, I may tell you, after a mere golden fleece, oh no! Orpheus. I wonder what happened to him…'

'Stoned and drowned,' said Odysseus helpfully. 'Dismembered at some stage apparently because of his insatiable appetite for young boys. There's a tomb on Lesbos where his head at least is buried. It's an oracle I understand. It's the sort of thing my father King Laertes keeps telling me about whenever we get together. He was aboard *Argo* as well, remember.'

'Oh,' said Nestor. 'I see,' though it was clear he didn't see at all and despite his sharp mind, he had forgotten he was talking to an Argonaut's son.

***

After an instant of hesitation, he continued, 'But while Orpheus was rhapsode on the *Argo*...' Then he went on to describe at some length the highlights of the voyage to Colchis, a voyage which by that time I had taken myself, alongside other merchants. As he told his story he added thoughts and comments about men he had known then whose reputations were generally fixed these days. Largely because most of them, like Orpheus, were dead. Captain Jason was crushed to death when part of the aged and rotting *Argo* fell upon him; Hercules ran mad in the end, killing two of his shipmates from the *Argo* the brothers Zetes and Calais, before he killed himself, convinced his clothes were magically setting his flesh on fire.

But while I entertained these thoughts beneath his rambling story, I took the opportunity to compare the two kings in more detail. Slim and sprightly, Nestor seemed always on the point of vigorous action, held in place only because he was talking. Even so, his hands flew like strange birds as he emphasised the action in his recollections with dramatic gestures. The breeze stirred his hair which curled to the collar of his tunic at the back. Enthusiastic spittle flew from the pale lips recounting his adventures, much of it lodging in the bushy beard, untidy as a heron's nest, that vanished down his neck and on beneath his tunic towards his chest. His eyebrows were as shaggy as the backs of mountain goats and as white as all the rest. Beneath them, his eyes gleamed a lively brown.

Odysseus was taller, broader, his body and limbs fuller, more muscular. His hands and feet were large, the former spare of gesture—as his orders were concise and to the point. His crew were so well-trained that he hardly needed to speak. With the sail still furled, the oarsmen eased the ship out of the harbour and up to the northern neck of the bay, then into the narrows which opened there, just wide enough to permit careful passage north between two headlands into another enclosed bay. At the far end of this, a second set of narrows finally opened out into the long, thin waterway leading northward still towards the coast of Thessaly and the port of Phthia dead ahead. Thessaly, Phthia, King Peleus, Prince Achilles and his war-winning army of Myrmidons.

As Captain Odysseus turned back from his impressively minimal ship handling, apparently paying the closest possible attention to King Nestor's reminiscences, those sea-bright eyes were everywhere—on the rigging, the rowers, the coast, the course. Once in a while his gaze would alight on me and the skin edging the corners of those piercing eyes would crinkle in secretly shared amusement.

Nestor's story also gave me time to think. I had travelled to Phthia often, though I had never met the elderly king, his impressive son, or his wife. I was used to coming this way—along the inner channel instead of going south and rounding the southern cape of Euboea Island, which stood now on our right, between us and the wider Aegean. My father's ships could reach Phthia in three days or so, depending on the wind and the current. But as my gaze followed the captain's I was struck by a simple truth. Father's vessels were fat, almost circular, with little difference between bow and stern. They had almost nothing in the way of oar power and relied on their sails. Captain Odysseus' ship *Thalassa* was long, shaped like a sword blade, and designed for speed. Twenty-five oars a side powered her independently of the wind, though a great square sail was furled against the yard, ready to be deployed if a wind came in behind us. Her lean flanks were caulked with pitch, making her long hull black, strong and resistant to leakage, worm, barnacles and weed. Where my father's ships were fully decked and designed with large storage areas below, this ship was only part-decked—the bow and stern were covered but a wide walkway rather than a full deck ran amidships past the mast, allowing the oarsmen light and air while they worked. But I reasoned there must be some storage room below as well, for arms, equipment, supplies.

The burden of all this was simply that whereas my father's ships would take three or four days to reach Phthia, I could confidently expect Odysseus, Nestor and the rest of us to be there some time tomorrow. I glanced back at the captain but his eyes were fixed dead ahead, on the mouth of the second narrows as Nestor told us all about the clashing rocks and how Jason had conned the *Argo* through them with the help of King Phineas of Arcadia and a dove. King Phineas who died stone blind and helpless not so long ago, I thought, happy that I was able to see that the ghost of the smile which we had shared still lingered on my captain's face.

iv

I soon found that Odysseus' thoughts on royal advisors were not the only area in which he departed from popular perceptions. He continued to say little but think a lot and that shared smile was the first of many we exchanged behind King Nestor's back. Not that he ever treated the old man with anything but respect and courtesy. Nestor was amongst the last, after all, of a legendary generation, many of whom, like Hercules, claimed direct descent from the gods themselves. But I knew he could see and share, perhaps, some of the frustration I felt when the first few lines of a song would be interrupted by a longwinded reminiscence that arose from them only tenuously but which silenced me and came close to driving my audience away altogether. Sometimes, as I listened, I imagined the crew leaping overboard rather than suffering any more—like Hercules' companion Hylas, supposedly seduced by water nymphs but certainly drowned in some lake or other long ago.

In due course, Odysseus would discuss with me some of the implications arising from his reluctance to follow the old ways of thought and forge new approaches to the situations he found himself confronted by in stark contrast to everything Nestor practised or advised. Early in our associations I also wondered why he chose to share his thoughts so openly with me. My father had explained some of the reasons he might have had for bringing me aboard, but I wondered at this unexpected openness, this intimacy between a king and a half-blind rhapsode—especially one who so rarely got a chance actually to finish a song. And the answer, turned out to be Telemachus. I was a temporary replacement for the son he loved so much that he gave up his feigned madness and agreed to follow Agamemnon when the child's life was threatened.

Long before he got the chance to have that discussion, however, the Fates gave him an opportunity to demonstrate his new way of thinking and reasoning.

It was approaching noon on the second day. We had overnighted ashore in a shallow bay on the west side of Euboea Island which we left soon after dawn and the oarsmen had settled into a good, easy rhythm a couple of hours earlier. They were powering *Thalassa* towards Phthia now despite the wind and an unexpectedly strong current running directly against us. The captain and King Nestor were at the stern looking back, discussing Agamemnon's best route when he had assembled his fleet and wanted to move against Troy. For once they were in complete accord. If he assembled them off Aulis, as Nestor said he planned to do, then he could lead them through the two sets of narrows we rowed through yesterday. But the counter-current we were facing now suggested to both of them that the narrows could all-too easily become a dangerous tidal race. Agamemnon would never get a thousand ships through it either swiftly or safely. No, they concluded. He would have to go south, round the southern end of Euboea Island and then turn north again, steering well clear of the dangerous Cape Kafirevs, oar-powered warships leading the fat supply ships with their big square sails. But he would only be able to do this if the winds were kind, blowing steadily from the south west for seven days or so.

The lookout on the forepeak broke into this lazy discussion. 'Something in the water dead ahead,' he called.

The captain and King Nestor walked the length of the ship with a briskness I could never match, so when I caught up with them standing in the bows looking down, I arrived part-way through another discussion. 'I do not advise it,' Nestor was saying, 'Think of the trouble Jason got into with bodies overboard as we escaped from Colchis with King Aeetes' gold and the Princess Medea, who, I have to say, makes Queen Thetis of Phthia look like gentle Aphrodite in comparison. Medea was terrifying even before Jason abandoned her in Corinth and went off with that pretty little thing Glauce. Dropping bodies into the water to distract pursuers, fine. Pulling them out again, not such a good idea in my experience...'

'...which is vast, old friend, yes I know. But there's something about this particular body... And, besides, just because he looks dead does not mean that he actually is dead.' Captain Odysseus raised his voice. 'Back oars! Steersman, get me as close to that piece of wreckage as you can. I'm going down for a closer look at the man lying on it.'

A few minutes later, as the ship heaved unsettlingly, the counter-current pushed what looked to me like a makeshift raft of splintered wood against her cutwater, just below the eye painted there. Captain Odysseus elected to go over and down himself. He looped a rope round his chest beneath his arms, tied it tight and Nestor reluctantly oversaw a team of crewmen holding onto it. Then, with easy athleticism, the captain swung himself out and over *Thalassa*'s side. Keeping his back to the water, he walked fearlessly downwards until he must have felt the spray from the restlessly pitching raft against the backs of his legs. Then he stepped down to stand upon it, riding its movement like an experienced horseman astride a fractious mount. He stooped over the splayed body, obviously trying to turn it over as green water washed over his feet and ankles. But this took a moment to do, for its belt was wedged under a sizeable splinter of wood. As soon as the body was free, the captain gestured and King Nestor threw him down a second rope which he looped round the body's chest.

'Is he dead?' shouted the king.

'Yes,' answered the captain. 'Very dead.'

'Then I'd advise you to leave well alone,'

'Too late for that now,' shouted Odysseus. 'There's

something about this particular corpse that interests me. Pull us both aboard!'

***

A few moments later, Odysseus laid the corpse out, face up, on the boards of the foredeck. Brine leaked off the dead man and his sodden clothing, making a considerable puddle. Two otherwise unoccupied sailhandlers helped, but it was the captain who did most of the work.

'Kings and heroes do not deal with dead bodies!' said Nestor disapprovingly.

'Except to create them,' observed Odysseus. 'And to take their armour as prizes in battle of course,'

'Work for women, common soldiers and slaves!' snapped Nestor and stamped away down the deck.

'Order us under way again, old friend,' called Odysseus after him. Then, dropping his voice and apparently speaking to himself, 'though you're right. We could probably use a woman or a house slave now.' He looked up at me with that conspiratorial smile. 'But as we have neither, I'll have to do my best.' He straightened and we stood shoulder to shoulder looking down. The sailhandlers stood back, ready for the captain's next command as the ship moved forward once again against that counter-current, surging towards Phthia.

The corpse was enough to give even a hardened soldier pause. It had only half a face. Dark hair swept forward over a pallid, wrinkled brow and over the stark white dome of a forehead half denuded of flesh. One eye and much of its nose were gone leaving great gaping pits. Its left cheek had vanished almost as far back as its ear, revealing a fearsome grin of yellow teeth poking out of ragged gums. Part of its chin was gone, giving another disturbing effect as the beard adorning what was left of the flesh on its right cheek swept forward over the naked left jaw like the fringe of its hair. The left side of its face was not all that was missing. Its left leg below the knee had also disappeared, the stump a pallid mess of waterlogged flesh and shards of bone. The rest was covered by a chiton tunic which seemed to be of good quality linen, cinched at the waist by a broad leather belt knotted firmly at the belly, though there were signs of strain both on the chiton and the belt itself. It was hard to tell much from the face, but the throat, arms and legs were all as white as marble—almost blue in tinge. It was a disturbing, unnatural colour. Odysseus crouched once more and began a minute examination of the dead man. He parted the remaining eyelid, opened both balled fists, examined the remaining leg and foot. Then he sat back on his heels deep in thought.

After a few more moments, he rose and gestured to the sailhandlers who stooped to help him turn the body over so that the captain could examine the back. I was struck once more by that pale white, bluish flesh, especially in the crook behind the right knee. There was no crook behind the left knee—merely that shattered stump. Odysseus grunted and reached for the back of the dead neck. There, under a mat of grey hair, was the knot of a thong that I had not observed. After an instant's hesitation he pulled out a slim-bladed bronze knife and cut it free. He tugged gently until two rings appeared from beneath the tunic through which the thong had been looped and looped again. He studied them thoughtfully for a moment then slipped them into the leather purse he carried at his belt. Apparently dismissing these from his mind, he leaned forward once more and it was obvious what had claimed his attention. There was a slit in the tunic, its edges frayed and lightly discoloured. He placed his knife so that the point was just inside the slit. 'A blade of the same width,' he observed. 'And probably of the same length.' The blade of his knife was perhaps twice as long as his hand. He glanced down at the one remaining foot with its worn leather sandal. Then he looked up at his silent helpers. 'Take the chiton off,' he ordered. 'Carefully.'

The men obeyed, turning the corpse on its side to untie its belt – a task complicated by swollen leather and slippery knots. Lying like that, it was almost possible to believe that there was nothing amiss with the face as it was presented in profile with the left side hidden. But as soon as the belt was free, the chiton slid off the marble-white body as easily as the skin off a shedding snake. One of the sailors reached for the dead man's loin cloth, but Odysseus stopped him. They laid the body back, face down, and stood clear, one with the belt and the other with the sodden tunic. The absence of the tunic revealed a slit in the left side of the corpse's back that seemed to match the hole in the chiton. The wound pouted slightly, its lips parted to reveal a deep dark throat that reached beneath the shoulder-blade into the dead blue barrel of the chest. The captain leaned forward and pushed the flesh on either side. The lips parted slightly and a stream of clear liquid came out immediately followed by a foam of bubbles.

Odysseus rocked back on his heels once more. 'Turn him over,' he ordered. 'But be careful not to disturb his loin cloth. The poor man has suffered enough indignities without that.' He swung round to face me. 'Well, boy, what do you make of it?'

'Nothing more than I can see, Captain.' I replied. 'We have here a man about whom we know nothing except that the gods struck him down, seemingly by causing him to be stabbed in the back, though for some reason I cannot fathom there seems to be no blood from the wound. No more than there is from his missing leg. Who he was and what he did before his death, why he died and how he ended up floating on a raft missing half a face or half a leg eludes me entirely. I'm sure that no-one under Olympus could ever know.'

'What if I told you I had answers to almost every question you might ask?'

'Were you anyone other than Captain Odysseus I would doubt you.'

V

'Diplomatically phrased,' laughed Captain Odysseus. 'Let us begin and see whether I can dispel those doubts.' He paused for a moment seeming to put his thoughts in order. 'We begin not with *who* he was—that may come later—but with *what* he was. This will explain why I called for your attention in particular. He was, like you, a rhapsode. Observe the knee above the missing left leg. It is twisted. The thigh above it is thin compared with that on his right leg. But the shoulder on that side—the left—appears stronger with calluses in the pit of the arm. Furthermore, the sandal that remains is unevenly worn. Although a shark or some similar beast has robbed us of proof-positive, it is clear to see that he was, like you, crippled. And, furthermore, using a crutch.'

'By no means every crutched cripple is a rhapsode, Captain,' I said, even though I was amazed by what he had observed—that I had overlooked—and what he had made out of his observations.

'True,' he answered. 'But there is more.' He leaned forward and parted the eyelids on that one remaining eye. The eyeball itself was covered in a milk-white cowl. 'Crippled and half blind—perhaps wholly so,' he observed. 'Though again, the seas have robbed us of proof-positive.' He gestured to the gaping pit on the opposite side of the dead face.

'That's easy to say, Captain, but…'

'Ah. The final proof to persuade the young sceptic. Look at his right hand and compare it with your own.' As I did so, he continued his commentary. 'You see the calluses on his fingertips and thumb? His are more developed, but, like yours, they come from plucking lyre-strings.'

I looked at Odysseus, simply stunned. Now that he mentioned it, I could see everything he described, and was convinced by the sense he had made of his observations. It all seemed almost childishly simple—I could hardly understand how I had missed so much that was so obvious to him. But he had only just begun.

'A rhapsode of experience, perhaps of standing—as the quality of his chiton might well prove. It certainly proves that he was stabbed in the back and almost definitely died from the wound. But where is the blood, I hear you say; when a man bleeds to death there is a lot of blood. And so there must have been. But as my wife and household servants would be quick to explain, the most efficient way to clean a garment of blood is to wash it in cold water. And it will not have escaped your notice that we fished him out of an entire Aegean Sea full of cold water. But we can take matters one step further, I believe, for the efficiency with which the sea has cleaned off all but the faintest trace of blood proves that he was stabbed and immersed immediately afterwards. The body is damaged, both historically and recently, but none of the damage suggests he was stabbed on a cliff-top and hurled over the edge. It is unlikely he was stabbed on a beach and swam out to deep water as he died—or that he was stabbed by a river and literally *washed* out to sea. No. He must have been stabbed aboard some vessel or other, therefore, and pushed overboard at once. A proposition further supported by the fact that he remained alive long enough to pull himself onto this raft that the Fates supplied for him, and to secure himself to it by anchoring his belt to the sturdy splinter that held him safe even in face of an attack by a shark. The fact that he could not pull the missing limb to safety further suggesting that it was crippled and not fully under his control. Let us hope that Poseidon looked kindly upon him and allowed him to die gently from the stab-wound before the shark arrived.'

The sea-blue eyes lost focus. He seemed to go into some kind of trance. 'But where was this fatal vessel when the rhapsode met his end? Just outside the channel beyond Euboea Island which lied close on our right hand. Either approaching or leaving Phthia, bound to or from Skyros.' He pulled the two rings out of his purse and held them up. 'We have here the seals of King Peleus and of King Lycomedes,' he said thoughtfully.

'But what was a common rhapsode doing with the seals of kings around his neck?' I wondered.

'Their presence suggests that he was not such a common rhapsode after all,' he answered. 'But let us not get too far ahead of ourselves, for the shark was not the only sea-creature that attacked him. Some thing or things had the opportunity and the leisure to eat half his face. The opportunity was clearly presented by his dead head lying half in and half out of the water. But the leisure...' He looked up at the two sailors who still stood holding the belt and the tunic. 'How long do you think it would take to reduce his face to what we see here?' he asked.

'At least two days,' offered the man with the belt.

'Three?' suggested the one with the tunic a little hesitantly.

'I agree. Three days. So our deceased rhapsode was stabbed and thrown overboard from a vessel heading one way or the other between Phthia and Skyros as it passed beyond the opening of the channel between the mainland and this island some three days ago.'

'But why?' I demanded. 'Why in the names of all the gods

kill a rhapsode?'

***

Odysseus paused. He took a long breath. 'You still do not understand.' he said sadly.

'What more is there to understand?' I asked.

'Almost everything,' answered Odysseus. 'Everything of real importance, certainly.' Utterly unexpectedly, he commanded, 'Sing me the epic song you were singing when we first met. The one about Hercules at Troy.'

'I will fetch my lyre…' I said obediently.

'No need for that,' he decided abruptly. 'Just sing.'

'*Sing, Muses of the anger of Hercules,*' I began, *'black and murderous, costing the Trojans terrible sorrow, casting King Laomedon into Hades' dark realm leaving his royal corpse for the dogs and the ravens.'*

'Stop!' he ordered and, when I had obeyed, he continued, his voice low, his brow wrinkled with thought. 'That's it,' he said. 'Word for word.'

'It is what I always sing,' I said, also frowning – but with confusion rather than thought. 'I wrote it and I learned it, just as I learned the songs that Stasinus taught me. Word for word.'

'And you still do not see,' he prompted gently. 'You do not understand the importance…'

'No, Captain.

He shook his head. 'That you, the youngest amongst us should share so much understanding—or lack of it—with the oldest. To King Nestor and men of his generation, things seem so simple. Because they only see surfaces. If a thing is then it is as it appears to be—no more and no less. Caused or created by the gods, immutable, unquestionable. They see no alternatives. They see everything face-on, no other possibilities admitted—or even considered. If they come up against a wall, they must either go over it or through it. They have no concept of finding a way *around* it.'

'Captain…'

He gave a sigh of frustration and his expression reminded me of my father's when he tried to explain something to his slow-witted children. 'Oh very well! Consider. You are King of

Phthia or King of Skyros. You know that the overbearing, unforgiving High King Agamemnon of Mycenae is gathering an army and will soon send emissaries to you demanding aid, troops and money. Like the King of Ithaca you cannot afford to have such a powerful man as your enemy. But you wish to consult your closest friend, a nearby king, before Agamemnon's messengers arrive. You need, therefore, to send a long, complex message and expect an equally lengthy reply—each one of which must be as dictated—word for word; perfect.

I nodded, understanding his point. The only type of record keeping other than a messenger's memory I had ever come across were the marks on clay tablets I had made under the tutelage of the Cretan record keeper in the warehouse at Chalcis and they were only useful for recording the details of ships' manifests and the contents of warehouses—unless one was a High King, immensely rich and powerful, keeping a scribe handy to aid communication with other High Kings like yourself.

'Who better to be your messenger than your rhapsode?' Odysseus continued. 'After all, his whole existence turns around learning one lengthy song after another—all word-perfect. Who else in almost any court of any king could be relied upon to learn and carry such a message? And, on his arrival be invited into the royal presence at once to perform his songs and entertain the court? How easy would it be therefore to pass on secret messages? As was, in fact done three or four days ago. Either King Peleus or King Lycomedes gave their rhapsode a message to be taken to the other. But someone knew how the message would be carried and wished to stop it. They went aboard with the rhapsode and whoever else was in the embassy if there was one, and at some point three days ago they stabbed the rhapsode in the back and pushed him immediately overboard. The rings identify the sender and the recipient of this lost message, but not which is which. However, if we wish to discover why the deed was done and learn, perhaps, who did it, we will find our answer at one court or the other. And we will start with Phthia of course, because both King Nestor and I have immediate business there.'

2 – Phthia

i

The harbour at Phthia was a wide bay with a sandy bottom that sloped up to a golden curve of beach. A jetty reached out from the heart of the beach like an arrow behind the curve of a flexed bow. Thick planks had been secured between wooden piles driven deep into the sea-bed, reaching far enough out for seagoing vessels to tie up against. At the landward end of the jetty there was a path across the sand beaten hard by passing feet, and beyond that a narrow roadway leading up the slope of a hill towards the walled town at whose centre stood a citadel crowned with King Peleus' palace. In the brightness of a clement afternoon, the white walls and red roofs gleamed hospitably. The marble porticoes of the temples offered comfortable shade from a sun struck, windless day. The gates of the citadel stood wide and the palace itself, walled and columned with the famous white marble of Thassos, seemed cheerfully welcoming. There was nothing sinister about the place at all.

The two kings strode down the gangplank and set off side by side, their entourage at their heels. Gifts and other necessaries followed close behind, mostly on the shoulders of the oarsmen. They all set a good pace up the increasingly steep thoroughfare—far faster than anything I could match, especially as I was laden with one bag containing my own immediate requirements and another which carried my lyre. In fact, the only person there moving more slowly than me was the murdered rhapsode. Odysseus ordered that he should be brought ashore with us and had caused him to be wrapped in a sturdy piece of linen kept aboard to mend the sail. Four men carried the corpse along the jetty, across the beach and up towards the gleaming palace which the captain calculated might well have been his home. However, if he proved to be a stranger here, he would be coming with us on the next leg of our journey. The captain had shared his thoughts with me as readily as he shared his smiles.

'Our mysterious guest must be familiar to one king or the other; perhaps both if he was a regular messenger between them. Let us begin by seeing whether he is Peleus' man. Knowing where he was coming from will help us discover who came with him. After all, the man who stabbed him is most likely to have been among his companions. You see the reasonable steps leading from one point to the other? In a sequence to which we might apply the term Logos, logic.'

I was indeed beginning to see the faintest glimmer of his new method of reasoning. I had been astonished by the effects he achieved by applying it to the dead rhapsode aboard his ship. The thought of observing him as he applied it to the mutilated corpse in the courts of two ancient kings while he attempted to unmask the poor man's murderer filled me with even more excitement than that which I had felt on first hearing Stasinus sing.

Phthia was not yet on a war-footing so the gates to the city and those to the citadel stood wide and the guards were almost friendly. The town between was a bustle of domesticity and commerce and the kings passed through without earning a second glance. Men and women came and went around us, most carrying baskets to and from the agora. The wares displayed at the market there emphasised a fact that I was already aware of—that the town relied less on imports carried up from the harbour and more upon goods and foodstuffs brought in from the fields and hills that lay behind the place. Fertile lands stretched almost as far back as Mount Pelion and what was grown there fed many of the cities along this coast.

The guards at the citadel gate had already been warned about my cloth-wrapped companion and so one of them unhesitatingly guided us across the palace courtyard and through a small side entrance, one of several leading off the modest, marble-flagged square. Having been given no other instructions, I followed the corpse. The palace was a relatively modest building from the outside, but the simple length of the corridor that led inward and downward allowed me to speculate that there was more to the place than met the eye. Beneath the striking hilltop stronghold there lay a maze of tunnels that would have challenged even Theseus had there been a Minotaur hidden somewhere within them. An apt enough thought, I calculated, because some years earlier King Peleus' close friend and confidant King Lycomedes had welcomed Theseus to Skyros, only to have the aged king tragically fall to his death off a cliff.

The tunnel, lit by occasional flaming torches in sconces along the walls, led past the openings of other tunnels and, between these, one dark cell-like room after another, many prepared as makeshift sleeping chambers with beds, tables and lamps, all currently unlit. This was unusual enough to draw my attention. Most of the palaces I knew of had large chambers or megarons which served as dining halls by day, places of feasting and entertainment in the evening and dormitories by night. The only palace I could think of that shared this unusual design was King Priam's palace at Troy; soon to be sacked and razed to the ground if High King Agamemnon got his way. After the welcoming warmth of the afternoon above-ground, the tunnel we were following seemed chilly and dank. There was a dead smell to it—of damp rock and old smoke. I shivered—as much at my gloomy thoughts as at the atmosphere which must be one of the most unsettling in any palace. But then, I thought, I had yet to visit King Lycomedes' palace on Skyros. Perhaps that too would seem more welcoming on the surface than it proved when you went further in. It never really occurred to me to wonder how King Peleus had known to have the extra accommodation prepared. Nestor and Odysseus had sent ahead no warning of our imminent arrival.

Beyond and below the sleeping chambers there were store rooms but they all seemed empty of people at the moment, if well-stocked with provisions. Our guide passed all this without comment—as taciturn as our cloth-wrapped companion. Eventually we arrived at small room that contained nothing more than a table and a couple of lamps with flames high enough to illuminate it. Odysseus' sailors put the corpse on this and stood back. Our guide then led us outward and upward. I found that, had I been Theseus myself, I would have needed neither Ariadne nor her thread. Theseus of course discovered he no longer needed Ariadne almost immediately after he had used her to aid his escape. He abandoned her on the island of Naxos, leaving her on that deserted lump of rock friendless and alone until she grew desperate enough to hang herself. Perhaps, I thought, he deserved that last long drop the Fates had in store for him on Skyros after all. In the meantime, it seemed to me that I could see the pattern of the tunnels like a picture in my head, far more clearly than I could see the real world around me. By the time we returned to the courtyard, I was confident I could find my way through them once again. In the courtyard we were greeted by a tall, clean-shaven, well-dressed man whose aristocratic features and air of decisive command marked him both as a nobleman and as a soldier. 'Where is it?' he demanded of my guide.

'In one of the cellars, Lord Hypatios,' answered the guard.

***

Lord Hypatios looked around the courtyard, then summoned a couple of men from the unit guarding the gate. 'You will take me back to where it is,' he said to the man who brought us out of the maze of corridors. He turned to the first of the gate guards. 'You will take Captain Odysseus' crewmen to the kitchens. There is food being served there.' He turned to the second. 'And you will take the rhapsode to the king.'

Lord Hypatios followed our erstwhile guide back the way we had just come. The first guard took Odysseus' sailors in tow and headed one way. The second one looked at me and jerked his head, indicating that we should go another way entirely. Without a word, he set off and I had no option other than to follow him. Less than pleased to be missing out on a meal that the sailors were enjoying, nevertheless I limped after him as quickly as I could.

Once again, the passages which he led me along fell into a simple pattern in my mind, and I was by no means surprised to find that they lead to the megaron or main hall. Here there was also feasting in progress – something I had divined some way back because of the odour of roasting goat which hung so fragrantly on the still passage air and the diffuse rumble of many overlapping conversations that accompanied it. The three kings, their senior advisors and retainers were gathered round a long board lined with platters piled with olives, eggs, cheeses, carrots and cucumbers. This table stood along one wall of Peleus' great hall or megaron with its ornate floor and ceiling, its painted walls depicting scenes from a boar-hunt and colourful columns standing at the corners of a great square opening above the blazing circle of the central fire-pit.

As well as the fragrant goat, there was a dolphin being cooked over the fire. Slaves were moving to and fro between the diners and the cooking fire, serving King Peleus and his guests with slices of steaming meat, reaching across at their direction to add eggs, olives, cheeses or vegetables to the flat loaves and terracotta plates before them. Yet more were circulating assiduously with amphorae of wine and water. 'Ah,' said Odysseus, looking up, 'here he is at last.' He moved slightly to reveal an empty place at the table beside him. I hesitated, until King Peleus himself gestured at the vacant seat. 'It's the rhapsode's place, reserved for you. Please be seated.' My hesitation gave me the chance to make one simple observation before the King spoke. There were no women at the table, or indeed anywhere in the room—only men.

'After you have eaten and drunk, you may sing for your supper,' said Odysseus. He shot a meaningful glance across the table at Nestor and, as I sat, sipped water and nibbled a slice of goat with a small cucumber and an olive or two, all-but overcome by the company in which I found myself. I was racking my brains to think of a song that would not be guaranteed to call forth a story from Nestor after the first line or so but Odysseus interrupted my chain of thought almost immediately. 'It's lucky we had you aboard,' he said in a tone so innocent that it should have aroused my suspicions immediately, 'King Peleus was just explaining that his rhapsode is away at present.'

'It is an honour to be asked to perform before such a company,' I said, too preoccupied to register his tone or his speaking look.

'Don't be shy, boy,' said King Peleus. 'You'll be lucky to

outshine Dion my rhapsode, but you can try. You'll be better than nothing at least'

I'm sure he meant the words kindly but of course they simply made me more nervous still. I felt Odysseus stir at the rhapsode's name, however, and caught up with his thinking then. Dion. It looked like we knew who the corpse in the little store room was. Where he had come from, therefore, and where he was going to when he met his end. Another step or two, perhaps, along the road of logic towards the unmasking of his murderer.

After the feasting was finished, the drinking continued. There was a strange air of freedom about it all, as though the king and his courtiers were children released from school; or as though the didaskalos schoolmaster with his cutting words and stinging birch rods was away for the moment. It infected their guests. The conversation grew increasingly loud as it flowed this way and that.

'And your son, Prince Achilles?' asked Odysseus. 'Is he not joining us?'

'He's away,' answered Peleus. 'Both Achilles and his companion Patroclus son of Menoetius, King of Opus.'

'Both Prince Achilles and Prince Patroclus are away?' wondered Odysseus as though he did not fully understand.

'Patroclus is no longer a prince,' snapped Peleus, his tongue loosened perhaps, by the wine. 'He lost his right to that title along with the love of his father and the respect of his people when he committed murder.'

'Murder?' wondered Odysseus. 'He committed murder and yet you allow him to be companion to your son? Are you not worried?'

There was a moment's silence, then Peleus gave a dry laugh that sounded to me like the rattling of long dead bones. 'There is nothing to fear. Achilles can take care of himself better than any man in Greece. Better, perhaps, than any man alive.'

ii

'Achilles and his companion have returned to our old didaskolos Chiron on Mount Pelion, perhaps?' probed

Odysseus, who, like Peleus and many other aristocrats. had been tutored by the wise old scholar at one time or another. He did not ask for any details about who Patroclus had murdered, when or where, suggesting to me that he already knew the facts of the matter and was hunting different game.

'Perhaps. Chiron is always busy teaching someone something.' Peleus was abrupt; making no secret of the fact that he was unhappy to be discussing the subject of his son and his murderous companion. His abruptness almost concealed the fact that he was also being suspiciously evasive. Had he not been our host and a widely respected monarch, I might almost have thought he was lying. 'Perhaps it is time for the rhapsode…' he continued.

But this time it was King Nestor who interrupted him. 'And the queen? Is the lovely Queen Thetis not to join us?'

'The Queen is of the old school,' prevaricated Peleus. 'She and the women eat when we men are finished.'

'Her women,' probed Odysseus once more with a shake of his head denoting his surprise. 'I have seen neither Queen Thetis nor her handmaidens. Not a woman in the place, unlike in the town itself. No wives to your courtiers, slaves, servants or chambermaids. Are you telling me that you have built women's quarters since I last visited, so that you can hide your women all away in the eastern fashion like King Lycomedes does on Skyros? You'll be telling me you've set up a harem like King Priam in Troy next!'

'No, no,' answered Peleus uneasily. 'Queen Thetis is also away. On a visit. Her most immediate companions are with her.' He took a deep breath Just for a moment I founmd mysef wondering whether the air of freedom pervading the megaron had anything to do with the fact that Queen Thetis was absent. But King Peleus overrode such thoughts at once. 'Enough of this,' he said. 'I will hear your rhapsode singing now.'

And that was that.

Or it would have been had not Lord Hypatios returned at that moment. As I eased myself off my chair and began to cross the room to the rhapsode's stool which stood in its traditional place beside the fire pit, I observed Hypatios out of the corner of my least damaged eye. He walked purposefully along the table until he was standing beside the king. He leaned forward and whispered at some length into the king's ear. After a while, King Peleus raised his right hand a finger's length off the table. It was a tiny gesture but it stopped all movement and conversation in the room. 'I asked Lord Hypatios to look at the body King Odysseus so bravely rescued from the grip of Poseidon,' he said. 'I admit I was worried that it might be my rhapsode Dion who I sent as embassy to King Lycomedes of Skyros. I am assured, however, that he is not Dion but a stranger. He has never been a member of my court. Never, as far as Lord Hypatios knows, even been a visitor here.'

Peleus paused to look around the room. He straightened. His shoulders squared. A subtle but impressive change came over him. His gaze was suddenly that of a legendary king and hero. He was for a heartbeat the fabled hero Peleus, son of Aeacus—the deadly warrior who, with his elder brother Telemon, had helped crew the *Argo*, had hunted the Calydonian boar in Hercules' absence, who had murdered his own half-brother Phokos and his father-in-law Eurytion, causing the suicide of his first wife, and slaughtered the hated Queen Astydamea of Iolcos by chopping her into pieces and marching his army between her scattered limbs to conquer and sack her country. 'It is time to hear the rhapsode sing,' he snapped.

I limped on across to the rhapsode's stool and sat there, pulled my lyre from its bag and settled it on my lap, wedging it in place with the club of my left arm, taking firm hold with my left hand. I ran the fingers of my right hand over the strings, unnaturally aware of the calluses on my fingertips and along the side of my thumb. Fighting against a shiver as I compared myself unsettlingly with the dead rhapsode in the tiny room far below. My audience quietened expectantly. The last face I saw before I closed my eyes to aid my memory, was Nestor's. I imagined him to be preparing yet another reminiscence likely to be fatal to whatever I tried to sing. I took a breath and sent a swift prayer to Apollo, god of poetry and song, that I had outfoxed the old man and would manage to keep a high dam standing in front of the overwhelming flood of his recollections.

'You lower gods, served by the numberless host of the dead,' I sang, *'into whose greedy coffers is paid the golden soul of every man that dies upon the earth; you whose fields are bordered by the pale streams of the intertwining River Styx, unfold for me now the mysteries of your sacred tales and the secrets of your world so far beneath the world of living men...'*

'Good choice of song,' said Odysseus later, when the song was over—the applause had died, the feast was breaking up, and the guests were being led towards their sleeping-quarters while the first of the women of Queen Thetis' court came in to have their supper and tidy up after us. 'I don't think King Nestor has ever sat silent for so long. Pretty apt in subject matter too, given our current mission. Just think how easy it would be if you really could get down to the banks of the River Styx and talk to the spirits of the dead on the other side. If we could do that, we'd find out whether our murdered corpse really is Dion in spite of what King Peleus and Lord Hypatios say. And who stabbed him in the back. All in a couple of heartbeats. Not that the dead have heartbeats—or hearts, I suppose.' He shrugged, then he winked. 'In the meantime, we'll just have to use our ingenuity. And maybe a bit of logic.'

He paused in the doorway looking back as the women silently filed in and their female slaves got ready to serve them with the parts of the goat and the dolphin that the men had not consumed. At least there were fresh eggs, cheese, olives and cucumbers, I noticed. 'Is this usual?' I asked quietly. 'I have only seen separation such as this in the cities of the east.'

'It certainly isn't an Achaean tradition,' he answered, but his tone was distracted. 'They'll be wearing veils next!' Abruptly he left me and crossed decisively to the table where a small group of women were gathered around one particular companion. This was a woman who appeared to be of middle age. She was dressed in dark robes in contrast to those of her companions. Odysseus exchanged a word or two with her then returned to me, frowning. 'That is Evadne,' he said abruptly. 'Wife to the rhapsode Dion. I asked her to describe him to me as I don't remember him from previous visits here myself. Hard to be certain about our corpse, in any case—not with half his face gone. Perhaps only a wife or mother would recognise him now.' He lapsed into silence as he led me out into the palace's passageways and through to the bed chamber he had been assigned. 'I've asked for a spare pallet to be put in my chamber tonight,' he said. 'You'll be sleeping on that. We'll have work to do before dawn.'

***

'Time to be up and about, boy.'

I opened my eyes and could just make out the figure of Odysseus towering by my bed, shielding the flame of a lamp he was holding. There was sufficient light for him to cast an enormous shadow on the wall and ceiling behind him. I pushed aside the cloak I was using as a blanket, rolled over and began pulling myself to my feet. 'Where are we going, Captain?' I asked.

'Exploring,' he answered. 'I want to test some of the things King Peleus said at dinner. I'm pretty certain he was being deceitful. I just don't know how much deceit was involved and about what.' He gave a dry chuckle. 'And I want you there to protect me if he was lying about Queen Thetis being away and we suddenly bump into the old gorgon.'

'Is she really that frightening?' I asked as I stood up and adjusted my tunic.

'Let's hope you never find out,' he answered in a cheerful whisper as he turned to lead me out of the doorway.

We were housed in the main palace, in rooms only slightly less sumptuous than the king's. 'These rooms probably belong to senior courtiers such as Hypatios,' said Odysseus as we crept along the passageway between them. 'They'll have been demoted to make room for us and their underlings will consequently have moved down too. Probably to the rooms along that corridor you have already described to me, which they'll share with the attendants Nestor and I brought with us. We'll have to move like ghosts and pray they sleep like the dead.' He paused, then added in a pensive whisper, 'I'm surprised Peleus managed to get them ready in time, though. It's as though he was expecting us. And we didn't send word ahead on purpose. We didn't want the old king to have time to prepare...'

'Sleeping arrangements?' I suggested when his voice tailed off.

'That and much more,' he answered. Then he was in motion again.

It was precisely as he said, I thought. The rooms along the passage I had seen earlier were obviously for visitors' personal retainers and lesser courtiers. Our crewmen would be sleeping aboard the ship or in a camp on the beach beside her. Having committed the layout of the upper palace to my memory, I had little trouble in guiding the captain out to the courtyard. We met no-one on the way, but as soon as we stepped out into the moonlit space, a couple of sleepy guards stationed by the main gate turned and looked at us suspiciously. Odysseus allowed the brightness from the lamp to light his features and the guards nodded in recognition, turning back to their other duties. 'Notoriety can sometimes be useful,' he said and handed the lamp over to me. 'Lead on.'

In fact I didn't need the lamp after we had crossed the courtyard, for the passageway down which I had followed the rhapsode's corpse was dimly lit by occasional, guttering torches. I handed the lamp back. Captain Odysseus took it and providentially left it alight. We proceeded as quietly as possible, therefore, staying as clear of the doorways into the sleeping chambers as we could and hesitating at the junction of each side-tunnel, his hand on my shoulder, until he was certain that no-one else was coming our way. We went on tip-toe, though to be fair we could have marched down the corridor leading a phalanx of Myrmidons and the noise would still have been covered by the storm of snoring we were creeping through.

As we eased forward from shadow to shadow, Captain Odysseus gave every appearance of being calm and confident, attributes I would have given anything to share. My chest was pounding as though there was an animal in there trying to escape. Soon I was gasping as though I had run from Marathon to Athens. My skin was oozing moisture almost as liberally as that of the dead rhapsode when the captain first laid him on the deck. The flashes round the edges of my vision were all too easily misinterpreted as the torches and lamps of guards coming to arrest us. I was so taken with this idea that at the crucial moment I failed to discriminate between what was happening behind my eyes and what was happening down the last of the side tunnels. Odysseus' fist closed on my shoulder almost painfully. He swept me by main force across the corridor and into the nearest room. As the Fates would have it, this was one of the store rooms, a convenient place for us to hide as the captain peeped round the edge of the door-jamb to see who was creeping along the tunnel towards us.

After a moment, a hunched and cloaked figure emerged, carrying a lamp which was shaded by one hand so closely that the palm must be blistering with the heat. The captain nodded silently as though he had expected to see what he was seeing—as he probably had. We watched as the figure crept along the corridor towards the store-room where the body lay. Odysseus tensed to step out of the doorway but before he could actually move forward, he stopped again and stepped back instead, pushing me into the darkest corner. He stood in front of me, his hand as close to the lamp's flame as the hunched stranger's had been. I did not have to wait long before I understood his sudden reversal. Two more figures strode past the doorway, one of them carrying a flaming torch rather than a puny lamp. Whoever they were, these men were not concerned about being discovered. They were not concerned about being followed either, as we discovered when we craned round the edge of the doorway then stepped back out into the corridor a safe distance behind their backs.

'That's Lord Hypatios with the torch,' breathed Odysseus. 'And that's King Peleus with him. Just as I expected.'

iii

'But you said it wasn't him! You lied!' The voice echoed out into the corridor where Odysseus and I were standing. The words were spoken in a woman's voice; low—almost a whisper—but throbbing with outrage and grief.

Although the woman was speaking in low tones, Lord Hypatios nevertheless snarled, 'Be quiet! Someone will hear!'

'You *lied*!' repeated the woman in a voice that was indeed quieter, but no less outraged.

'Evadne,' said King Peleus, unexpectedly softly. 'Lord Hypatios did not lie. He whispered the truth to me. It was I who lied.' His confession should have enraged the woman further, but the tone of his admission seemed to soothe her. And it was the king who had lied, after all.

'You lied, Majesty? But why?' there was genuine shock in her voice now.

'You must see,' he continued overriding her question, 'how careful we must be. Especially with yet more of the High King's emissaries here. Agamemnon is a suspicious man, quick to take offence and slow to forgive anything he believes to be an insult or a betrayal. If he suspected for a moment that secret messages were circulating in the face of his call to arms, that there are plans being prepared to hide from him the soldiers he wants to lead on his mad enterprise…'

'At the very least,' soothed Hypatios, 'it would be a distraction from the more important task the Fates have given us: to find and punish whoever did this to Dion.'

'That's what all this secrecy and deceit is about is it?' hissed the rhapsode's widow, unconvinced, 'finding out who's responsible for my husband's death? How ironic, when we know precisely who is responsible!'

'And who might that be?' demanded Peleus, and suddenly his voice was no longer so reasonable. It was the voice of a man who had led an army through the scattered remains of a queen he'd just chopped to pieces. The rhapsode's widow might well be risking her liberty if she persisted with this, perhaps even her life.

'Whoever gave him the fatal message in the first place!' she spat nevertheless.

'Or,' suggested Hypatios immediately, 'whoever caused the circumstances which made the secret messages so necessary.'

'You mean to blame Agamemnon for this?' her tone was incredulous. 'My Dion was simply the first casualty in the war he plans against Troy? Is that what you're suggesting?'

'No, Evadne,' said the king, his tone placatory once again.

'The responsibility for the murder as well as for the lies is mine and mine alone. You go back to bed now and rest assured that I will discover who did this and why. Then I will make them regret it until their dying day; which may in fact arrive sooner than they think.' There was a whisper of footsteps as the woman obeyed her king's direct order. Odysseus tensed, ready to pull us back out of sight, but he was far too late. Providentially, however, the woman turned back in the doorway to address the king once more. 'You swear this, Majesty? That whoever did this will pay?'

The question gave us time to hide ourselves in the last store-room before the one containing the corpse. We watched the distraught woman retrace her steps. King Peleus and Lord Hypatios waited in silence until the last glimmer of her lamp had faded. 'But you did give Dion a message, Majesty,' said Hypatios. 'One that will not now be delivered. Was it vital?'

'I thought so,' answered the king but his tone was distant, like his mind, evidently, because he suddenly changed the subject. 'I gave him more than a message. I gave him the ring that bears my seal – and Lycomedes' ring as well. They are both gone.' There was a heartbeat of silence. Then the king continued, his voice thick with suspicion. 'Does the murderer have them, or does Poseidon—or does Odysseus?'

'If Odysseus has them then he also knows you lied, Majesty. And he may have shared that knowledge with King Nestor.'

'And if they know that, they may carry the information back to Agamemnon, might they not? Unless we can think of a way to stop them.'

'A dangerous thought, Majesty. Neither one will be easy to silence, if your plans were to run that way.'

'Perhaps they do; perhaps they do not. We will invite them to stay for at least one more day, while we consider the best way forward. First thing in the morning I want you and General Argeiphontes to parade the force from my army that we were thinking of sending to Agamemnon.'

'Yes, Majesty.'

'And send a message to Generals Menesthos and Eudorus. I want the Myrmidons up and out on parade as well.'

***

'That's a bit worrying,' said Odysseus—though he didn't actually sound particularly worried. 'I know Nestor and I have a bit of a reputation—but two full armies to come against us. And one of them made up of Myrmidons! I think even the old man and I would have our hands full there!' He stepped out of the little room and looked up the black throat of the corridor just as the brightness of Hypatios' torch was snuffed out because the king and he had turned a distant corner. We ourselves set out to return, conducting our conversation in whispers as we went.

'But King Peleus said he wanted you to stay for one more day, not for the rest of eternity!' As I followed my captain, my voice shook with the worry he so obviously did not feel. I was beginning to regret my song about the underworld and how easy it was even for god-like heroes to find themselves on the far bank of the River Styx.

'Don't worry, lad. If we can't outfight him, I'm sure we can find a way to outfox him! Besides, I think I want to talk with General Eudorus. Everybody has been very careful not to talk about him, but there's been another envoy from Agamemnon visiting here ahead of us. Even something as simple as the preparation of these rooms suggests it. But if he *was* here, Eudorus will tell me, soldier to solder.'

'Another envoy, Captain?' I asked. Agamemnon *really* did not trust Odysseus, I thought.

But Odysseus didn't answer my question. Instead he asked another of his own. 'I wonder, have Peleus and Hypatios drawn the other more worrying conclusion from Dion's death now that they have registered and admitted it?'

'What is that Captain?' I asked.

'Yet another sequence dictated by logic,' he answered. 'We brushed against it earlier, but now, I think, it is time to consider it more fully. The rhapsode Dion was given a message to carry from Peleus to Lycomedes. It was the first time he had done so, perhaps, as he carried the royal seals to prove his function; or at least to ease his passage through the royal court of Skyros. Agreed?'

'Yes, Captain.'

'A message almost certainly to do with Agamemnon's summons to arms; presumably arising from the visit of the first emissary. Almost certainly to convince Lycomedes that Phthia and Skyros should co-operate in some manner to thwart the High King—or at least to adapt his orders to their own convenience. As, to be fair, they must already do—Lycomedes is king of the Dolopians and would need to lead them into battle alongside troops from Skyros if he joins Agamemnon.'

'I see…' I said.

Odysseus disregarded my less than certain tone and continued down his path of logic.

'The Dolopians, however do not live on Skyros—not many of them at any rate. Although they accept Lycomedes as their king, they actually live here in Phthia. Dion the messenger, therefore, was put aboard one of Peleus' ships, bearing a very lengthy and complex message to do with Phthians and Myrmidons as well as Dolopions and soldiers from Skyros!'

'I see,' I said again, with more certainty this time.

'But—and this is the heart of the matter, I think—someone stabbed Dion in the back and pushed him overboard.'

'We know that! We've known for more than a day…'

'Someone from the crew who must have been ordered to protect the messenger carefully. Someone he trusted himself—to have allowed to come that close to him. A dagger's length away or less. Don't you see where the logic leads? There is someone in Peleus' court—someone on the mission to Skyros—who is secretly working against him. Someone employed by Agamemnon, perhaps, or even Priam of Troy.'

'A kataskopos!' I whispered. 'There's a spy!'

'More than that, lad,' he answered. 'There's a dolofonos; an assassin.'

iv

We woke early next day and, having completed our ablutions, we went to the king's great megaron hall where Peleus himself was overseeing a breakfast of barley bread and olives with wine and water. Even Nestor was content to sit and eat, without discussing the many breakfasts he had enjoyed with Jason and the heroic crew aboard *Argo*. Instead there was the sort of conversation that one might hear round any table early on a summer's morning.

The informality did not last long. Lord Hypatios arrived with two men I guessed to be Generals Argeiphontes and either Menesthos or Eudorus. One decisive and commanding man dressed in dazzling bronze, the other, equally commanding, armed in black. One from the Phthian army, therefore, and the other from the Myrmidons.

'Your majesties, my lords,' said Hypatios, 'It is the wish of King Peleus that you be invited to witness a display of military manoeuvres. Generals Argeiphontes and Eudorus will each lead their men in a martial exhibition and then, later, in a mock battle which the three kings are invited to judge as to which would be the victor in actual combat.'

There was a moment of silence, then Nestor said, 'Of course I once witnessed just such a battle between Hercules' heroes and the Amazons. Though I have to say the outcome fell under the aegis of Eros and Aphrodite rather than Ares and Athene. What happened was this…'

'We would be honoured!' Odysseus cut him off. 'To witness the Myrmidons in action, even in the absence of Prince Achilles their commander. For an experience such as that we would be happy to delay our mission by, let us say… A day?'

'I wonder what he's up to,' said Odysseus as we all dutifully followed our host and his generals out of the palace some time later.

'Do you think it could be some kind of a trap, Captain?' I wondered nervously.

'Possible but unlikely. If he does decide to move against us he's probably too wise to do it here. If I was him and I wanted to get rid of us I'd do something to the ship so that we sank and drowned somewhere between here and Skyros.'

'But the fact that Dion didn't drown and we found him afloat shows that such a plan is not guaranteed of success.'

'True, lad! Well observed. We'll make something of you yet! To be certain-sure, Peleus would have to send a ship to shadow us until we sank. One whose crew could be counted on to make certain that none of us was ever found afloat. Or of course he might have an assassin of his own who could come aboard and stab a few backs, slit a few throats…'

'And could he do that?' My voice shook with horror at the thought. 'Send a ship after us to sink us and slaughter us?'

'He's a king and a general,' answered Odysseus. 'To stand any chance of doing that he'd need to be a king and a captain. And a better captain than I am—not to mention the fact that I have King Nestor who crewed the *Argo* to help and advise me!'

That cryptic remark brought our conversation to a close.

The rear sections of Peleus' palace did not open onto a courtyard as the forward sections did. Instead, a gate almost as massive as the Scaean Gates of Troy led out onto a roadway which in turn ran inland towards a broad flat space clothed with short-cut grass. Straight ahead, it seemed to stretch for at least a dolichos mile, maybe two, before the lower slopes of a range of hills. These rose, tree-clad, as foothills to the more distant mountains, and eventually to Mount Pelion itself. Side to side it was wider still, or would have been but for the military encampments that had been erected on either hand to house the soldiers of the Phthian army and the Myrmidons. The grass in the centre was bruised and muddied by the soles of countless boots and ridged with wheel-marks. On the near-side of this, standing with its back to the palace there was a tiered grandstand which had clearly been erected so that an audience could observe the manoeuvres and the mock battle due to follow them.

'This didn't go up overnight,' said Odysseus.

'No it didn't' agreed King Nestor as he joined us. 'I wonder what his game is.'

'It's a game he's played to an earlier audience,' said Odysseus. 'Did Agamemnon send anyone out ahead of us to prepare the ground as far as you know, Nestor?'

'I remember when Hercules and I scouted the Isle of Lemnos ahead of Jason and the others before they came ashore…' said Nestor, seemingly losing focus on present reality once again. Odysseus frowned, but I could not tell whether it was a grimace of irritation, anger, frustration or suspicion.

But then the time for conversation was past. King Peleus mounted the stand, easing himself into a throne secured in the best position. Nestor and Odysseus were invited to sit on either side of him and the rest of us took our places depending on rank and standing. As I searched for my seat, I noticed that Odysseus' seat was larger than Peleus' throne, seemingly made for a man whose stature was even greater than my captain's; a man of almost gigantic proportions. Frowning with thought, my forehead no doubt as wrinkled as the pensive Odysseus', I turned back to search for my place. Despite my position as stand-in rhapsode I was lucky not to be sitting on the grass. Not that it would have mattered. The moment the display began I was simply transported.

***

It began with the chariots. Out of the centre of each line of tents came a lone chariot. Each one was pulled by a magnificent pair of horses, chestnuts for the army and black for the Myrmidons. Each chariot moved on spoked wheels whose upper rims might reach a tall man's waist. From what I could see of the chariot cars they were floored in wood and walled in ox-hide held firm by a wooden frame. In each chariot stood a charioteer who held the reins. Beside him stood his general—Argeiphontes in bronze and Eudorus in black. Each man had a shield hanging outside the car at his hip. Each man carried two tall ash-wood spears tipped in wickedly glittering bronze. You would have expected the chariots to come racing full-tilt at each-other, I certainly did. But no. The horses moved forward slowly, high-stepping, heads held up and nostrils flared, clearly aching to burst into a gallop but held in check by the skill of the charioteers. Then, as the two single chariots paced out onto the field of battle, so, behind them, moving under equally perfect control, came two more lines of chariots; one line on each side. There were too many to count, but they seemed to stretch along the sides of the encampments right down the length of the field. It was a stunning spectacle of absolute control. But then, at a shout from each general, the chariots hurled into motion, charging full-tilt at each-other. My eyes widened. My cheeks ran with tears as my damaged vision strove to take in every detail. There was no doubt in my mind that the chariots were about to crash headlong into each-other. But again, no. The leading chariots passed each other, their wheel hubs separated apparently by fingers' lengths. And the lines behind them thundered through each-other in the same way, went careering towards the opposing tent-lines; only to turn at the last moment, swing round, re-cross the field avoiding each other seemingly at the whim of the gods and careering back to their own lines.

But these were no longer tent-lines, for, while my attention had been focussed on the chariots, so spearmen had stepped forward, rank upon rank, reaching away into the distance. Each man fully armed, helmet crested with horsehair, cuirass and shield of bull's hide—brown for the army, black for the Myrmidons. Each man carried two spears, almost a ten-foot akaina in length. File after file marched out. Then, behind them the slingers and the archers, also in armour but with slings and bows instead of shields and spears. Once the bowmen were out, the lines stopped. By which time, the chariots were lined up in front of them again, horses sweating, steaming and stamping. 'They haven't organised all this overnight,' I said to myself, echoing the captain's observation. 'They've put this display on recently for someone else.'

This was a thought I held in mind while a small army of slaves and servants brought us lunch and the display was halted while we ate it, the soldiers standing at attention while the chariots wheeled round and vanished back amongst the tents behind them. The state of the muddied grass further emphasised to me that whatever I was watching now and destined to watch later, had been enacted before, perhaps a week ago. Maybe more, maybe less.

After everyone had eaten, drunk, performed any ablutions necessary, the exhibition resumed. From each army, a single soldier marched out of the tent lines and into the centre of the field. Each was followed by two more soldiers carrying a wooden target carved into the shape of a man. They wheeled round and marched away down the field, side by side until they were incredibly far away from the spearmen. They placed the targets and stood clear. Not clear enough by my calculation—

remaining dangerously close. The brown-clad spearman and his black-clad companion moved together like a man and his shadow. Two spears soared away down the field to smash side by side into the breasts of their targets. Again, they moved in unison. Again, the spears pierced the wooden breasts, side by side. The soldiers turned and marched back to their ranks. They were replaced by two more spearmen. These were expert with the spear and shield. Face to face, they fought each other to a standstill, neither able to gain the upper hand. They were replaced by swordsmen, again, equally matched. Then dagger men. Then wrestlers. Then the targets were replaced, their spear-wounds made vivid by the splinters of white wood surrounding them. The archers sent their arrows unerringly at the targets' faces. The slingers smashed lumps of wood out of rough-hewn heads and chests.

v

After the individual displays came the mock battle. The two generals began it once again, their chariots charging at each-other then swinging to a halt at the last possible moment as the warriors leaped down, grabbing shield and spears. The first spear was thrown, each missing its target by a hair's breadth. The second was used in hand-to hand combat. And as the two leaders fought, every movement as carefully controlled as the most complicated dance, so the ranks of the chariots reappeared and echoed their mock attack. How the soldiers' wild combat did not result in mass slaughter seemed simply to rest on the will of the gods. Finally they disengaged, leaped back into their chariots and retired into their encampments, passing as they did so, the ranks of the spear-men in the brown and black armour who came charging out of their tent-lines to put on a display that held the audience entranced. Spears flew and then were used in close combat. After the spears, bronze-bladed swords, then daggers, then fists and arms as the combatants wrestled each other to the ground. Arrows flew in high arcs from side to side of the field, falling harmlessly among the tents. Only the slingers were not deployed, their sling-shots invisible and wasted in what was so carefully calculated to be a martial spectacle.

By the time it was all over, the sun was setting. The exhausted soldiers lined up once more, their ranks reaching down the field of battle: slingers and archers behind foot-soldiers, behind lines of chariots with the two generals in front.

'Your Majesties,' called Hypatios. 'Would you kindly judge which is superior in the skills of war, the king's army or the prince's Myrmidons.'

The three kings put their heads together for a conference that was surprisingly short. Then Odysseus rose from that out-sized seat. 'It is our judgement,' he announced in a voice that must have carried to the furthest exhausted combatant, 'that there is nothing to choose between them. Both armies are equally outstanding in every regard.'

His announcement was met with cheering so loud that Agamemnon himself might have heard it in his palace in distant Mycenae and, as the Myrmidons beat their spear shafts against their shields, mistaken it for thunder. The soldiers were dismissed and retired to their camps. The grandstand emptied slowly, the audience in pairs and groups discussing what they had seen, commenting on elements that had particularly impressed them. King Peleus led the way back into the palace. Hypatios announced that there would be time for everyone to cleanse themselves, then dinner would be served. But, again, I had already realised that. The whole place was aromatic with the scents of roasting ox and boar.

The huge animals had been turning on the spits for much of the day and yet there was still time for a lengthy wash and change of clothing—for those who had more than one outfit. As I followed Odysseus into the great hall having completed our ablutions, he said, 'Ah. That explains it. Of course.' Two more places had been laid at the great table and I was not surprised to see that they had been prepared for the two generals whose troops had put on today's breath-taking display. The lengthy hiatus between the end of the mock-battle and the start of the feast had been a simple courtesy—to allow the generals to wash off the sweat of combat and to change out of their armour. They came is shoulder to shoulder, but Argeiphontes sat at Peleus' right hand between Peleus and Nestor and was very much the king's favourite. This did not appear to upset Eudorus particularly, who seemed perfectly content to be seated on Peleus' left beside Odysseus. The captain also made room for me on his left, though my elevation to the royal group was even more daunting than my place lower down the table last night. But I soon forgot all about my nervousness as I eavesdropped on the conversation between my captain and the Myrmidon general who talked as though they were old friends.

As soon as Odysseus was certain that Peleus was concentrating on his general and his old shipmate from the Argo, he leaned across to Eudorus. 'That was a truly inspiring display,' he said. 'Was Prince Ajax equally impressed?'

***

'Ah,' said Eudorus, glancing across as his preoccupied monarch. 'You worked that out, did you? I think His Majesty's been trying to keep Ajax' visit a secret. He still is as far as I can see so you'd better not make too much of a fuss about it.'

'I'm not sure how serious he is about keeping it secret, though. Not when he leaves that massive seat on the grandstand,' said Odysseus. 'Still, I'll take your word for it: my lips are sealed—with Peleus and his court at least, if not with the occasional Myrmidon. But you must admit, Ajax was a far more logical choice of emissary than Nestor and me. He's the son of Peleus' older brother King Telemon of Salamis and Peleus' nephew therefore. *And*, of course, Prince Achilles' cousin. Cousin and close friend I believe. He should have had no trouble in getting both the king and the prince to fall in with Agamemnon's plans. And yet the fact the High King has sent us as well means Ajax' mission failed. What went wrong?'

'Prince Achilles wasn't here,' said Eudorus. 'It was as simple as that. He hasn't been here for a couple of months. Nobody knew where he'd gone to, except, perhaps, Queen Thetis and she wasn't about to tell. Things got quite heated in the end, the queen on one hand, the king on the other, Prince Ajax on the middle and Prince Achilles nowhere to be seen.'

'Heated? Why?' wondered Odysseus.

'As you say, Prince Ajax had come on the same mission as

you and King Nestor. To ask Prince Achilles to put the Myrmidons at King Agamemnon's disposal when he sails against Troy.'

'Yes. So?'

'Queen Thetis said that even though she had no idea where Achilles is, she nevertheless knows his mind in the matter. According to her, Prince Achilles does not want to join Agamemnon's army. He wants to stay in Phthia, get married, raise children, succeed his father in due course and rule his kingdom until his own son succeeds him.'

'She said that, did she? What did Ajax say?' I couldn't tell from Odysseus' tone whether he was surprised at Eudorus' words or not.

'He said she was wrong; that he knew his cousin better. That Achilles would do almost anything to bring the Myrmidons into battle. That he would rather die a hero and live in legend like Hercules than waste away and die an old man no-one would ever remember. Then he put the king on the spot and demanded to know his opinion. Peleus agreed with him that Achilles would join Agamemnon in the blink of an eye given the chance.'

'Queen Thetis won't have liked that!' Odysseus sounded surprised—at the old king's fortitude in the face of his wife inevitable outrage, perhaps.

'She banished Ajax there and then,' Eudorus explained. 'She swore everyone to secrecy from what I hear—a command that is beginning to fall apart in her absence. I have no idea what she said to the king later and I'm quite relieved about that, I must say. Anyway, what, three days ago, maybe four, she went off as well—no-one knows where. And no sooner had she gone than the king sent a fast ship to Skyros with Dion the rhapsode aboard. I'd guess he and she have been trying to hide the whole sorry business from you in a mixture of embarrassment and desperation.'

'I can see that. And I suppose the point of today's exhibition was to establish to us—as much as to Ajax when you first put it on—that the Phthian army which Peleus can control is every bit as good as the Myrmidons which only the missing Achilles can control. If we or Ajax can convince Agamemnon of that, then there's a chance he'll settle for general Argeiphontes and forget about Achilles altogether.'

'Yes; that's it exactly. We had to hold back and take it really easy on them, though. For the gods' sake don't tell General Argeiphontes or the king!'

***

I had become so engrossed in this conversation that, without thinking, I joined it. 'So many secrets!' I said. 'Surely it would be better to tell the truth about everything! Tell the king you know he's lying about Dion, that you think Ajax was right and Prince Achilles would rather die young and famous than live to old age in obscurity…'

I stopped, because Odysseus was chuckling indulgently—something my father used to do before saying something like, '*But you're too young to understand these things, lad. Maybe when you're older…*'

'Think,' said Odysseus. 'What is the likely outcome of telling a king to his face that you know he's been lying?'

'It would mean war,' said Eudorus.

'Right! War. Peleus against Agamemnon because we are his ambassadors. And Agamemnon wants war with Troy, not with Phthia. He'd find himself fighting Skyros too, as likely as not, with Peleus and Lycomedes being such good friends. And the Phthian army is pretty strong, as this afternoon proved, even if the Myrmidons were giving them an easy ride.'

'Moreover,' added Eudorus, 'If Peleus goes to war with Agamemnon, then Achilles is honour-bound to join him. As Peleus' son he'd have no choice. And that means the Myrmidons too!'

'The exact opposite of what the High King wants, what we were sent here to arrange,' said Odysseus. 'We'd be far better to say nothing, go our way and let old King Peleus save face. That way Agamemnon gets the Phthian forces while we try to find Achilles and arrange for the Myrmidons to join the High King too. We'll give poor old Dion a proper funeral in the morning and then be on our way.'

The conversation was interrupted by King Peleus.

'Rhapsode!' he shouted. 'Time to earn your supper!'

I limped over to the fire, sat on the stool there, and sang. '*Sing Goddess of the wedding of Ceryx and the heroic guests that attended there. Sing of the heart of the festival where the grandmother roasted so the people might feed. She laid down her strong brown daughters and let their tall golden children dance until all were consumed, going down to the grey...*'

'That was another very apt song you chose to sing last night,' said Odysseus next morning as we lingered on the beach while Nestor and his men got the ship ready to depart. 'Though you were lucky Nestor was too deep in conversation to notice the bit where Hercules came into it.' He was silent for a moment, looking pensively into the heart of Dion's funeral pyre. The morning wind blew cold across the bay, making the flames dance like naiads seducing Hylas to his watery death and roar like Nemean lions attacking Hercules. It was something he had arranged himself just as he had promised, out of respect for the dead rhapsode and in the hope it would comfort the grieving widow. Evadne, with some of her closest friends, was standing there beside us, tears running down her cheeks like molten gold in the pallid firelight. He had erected the pyre on the beach well within the view of the palace in case the king who said he didn't recognise the corpse might want to watch over the departing spirit of his murdered messenger. It was the closest he could come to calling Peleus a liar without starting a war.

'It's an allegory, that song,' he continued. 'The roasting grandmother is an acorn. Her daughters are branches from the tree she becomes and their tall bright children are the flames. And they all go down to the grey like the rest of us.' He lingered a few moments longer looking at the fire which was already ringed with grey ash then he turned to me and said, 'Skyros,' as though I hadn't already worked our destination out. 'We're off to Skyros now; I'm keeping Peleus' signet ring for the time-being but we have to check out Lycomedes.'

He turned right round to the jetty and as he did so, someone else came hurrying across the beach. I was dazzled by the brightness both outside my eyes and inside, so it took me a few moments to recognise the stranger. It was Lord Hypatios with a couple of personal servants laden with his gear. 'King Peleus wishes you to give me safe passage as far as Skyros,' he said.

I thought at once of what my captain had said about King Peleus sending someone aboard to stab our backs and cut our throats. But it seemed I was the only one harbouring such dark suspicions.

'Of course he does,' said Captain Odysseus cheerfully. 'Welcome aboard, my lord.'

3 – Skopelos

i

The presence of Lord Hypatios and his two servants made a marked difference to the atmosphere aboard Captain Odysseus' ship *Thalassa.* As well as those two grim-faced, sinister retainers, the tall aristocrat seemed to bring with him that air of equivocation, mystery and danger which haunted Peleus' court. It was clear enough that Hypatios was performing two functions—at least two, suggested Odysseus darkly, and maybe more. To begin with he must be carrying a simplified version of the secret message that Dion had committed to memory with such fatal consequences. Next, he was also almost certainly spying on us, and through us on Agamemnon and his preparations for war. Peleus and Lycomedes both almost certainly wanted more details of the High King's schemes, as well as lists of those lesser kings planning to bring their armies under his aegis or—perhaps more importantly still—those who might refuse to do so. But on the other hand, Odysseus was more than a little interested in the message Hypatios was carrying, and how that might affect his own recruitment drive, particularly in the absence of Achilles. It became a grim sort of game. Even the most casual remark which passed between the two kings and the Phthian lord became freighted with innuendo. The most innocent observation likely to be gutted in the search for double meanings.

Every now and then I seemed to see through the captain's eyes and understood that nothing in these conversations was as it appeared to be. Hypatios remarked upon the efficiency of *Thalassa*'s oarsmen—but was he really trying to discuss how Agamemnon was beginning to pull the Achaean kings together? He observed the strength of the current we were fighting—but did that mean he knew that the High King's plans were not proceeding as smoothly as he would like and was there a gathering movement pushing back against them? He praised the north wind blowing against our left shoulders and noted that it would help us when we finally began to run south—but did that mean he was thinking of the ease with which the northern islands might combine with the southern—Andros, Tinos, Syros, Paros and maybe even Naxos—if Skyros and Phthia led the way against the High King's peremptory demands? All this before we even began to approach the extra elements, beginning with my captain's off-hand remark of yesterday: perhaps Hypatios and his men were in truth seeking any opportunity to literally, actually stab us in the back or slit our throats as we slept.

The Aegean Sea did not help. Although the weather remained calm and clement with that promising northerly breeze kissing our left cheeks as we headed east between the southern coast of Thrace and the northern coast of Euboea Island, nevertheless we found ourselves fighting that surprisingly powerful current. On the one hand this was hardly unexpected—it was the current that had swept Dion's corpse on its makeshift raft down into the gulf and under our bows. But on the other hand, the tides in the Aegean do not rise or fall by much, so currents as fierce as this one were rare. Captain Odysseus shrugged fatalistically. We might be proceeding at our usual healthy pace under oar-power, he observed, but we were doing so over water that was sweeping us backwards almost as fast as we were being rowed forward. Even had this not been the case, Skyros was more than one day's sailing distant, so we would have to anchor somewhere convenient overnight before our final run south-east, hopefully with that steady northerly swinging westwards behind us.

By noon we were off the broad passage that led northward between two headlands into the great gulf named for Pagase, its main port. As Nestor was kind enough to point out at some length, it was at the shipyards of Pagase that Jason had *Argo* built, and from where he and his heroic crew set out on their voyage to Colchis. The tide turned as we passed the entrance to the gulf and began to push us eastwards so that by evening the grey and purple hump of Skiathos Island lay low on the northern horizon to our left as Captain Odysseus guided us into a welcoming bay on the south west corner of Skopelos Island with the sunset seeming to set the sea on fire behind us and turning the coastal hillside forest ahead of us to green-tinted copper and gold. I knew the place well, as did many mariners working up and down the islands along this stretch of the Aegean. It was a double bay separated by a low headland. The outer bay was a safe haven if the wind and weather turned foul, particularly as its beach sloped gently into the water so that it was possible to run your vessel right up onto the sand. However, the inner bay was safer still, surrounded by hills that stood against everything except a full-on westerly gale. Both bays provided popular places to overnight and to meet. They had a colourful history of secret assignations, smuggling and outright piracy. But that evening both bays seemed safe and innocent enough.

***

At first glance, the inner anchorage appeared quite similar to the port at Phthia but it had several major differences. The seabed here sloped steeply upward and if you looked over the bows it was possible to see a jumble of dangerous-looking rocks lying perilously close beneath the hull. The rising sea-bed paused for a moment at the tide-line to present a curve of golden sand—but *only* for a moment. Immediately behind the fingernail of beach, hillslopes climbed skywards on all sides, forested thickly enough to conceal an army of enemies and a menagerie of wild animals; forested far too densely to tempt anyone to clear space for a house, let alone a farm, village or town. I was among those who looked over the bows as we entered the bay because, like our team of sail-handlers, I was fishing for our supper. Between us we had a flapping and wriggling pile of red and grey mullet, bream and wrasse. I'd lost count of the fish we pulled up, but the pile reached higher than my knees. Even so, we would need more than that to feed fifty oarsmen, a dozen sailhandlers, the steersman and his two helpers, the two kings, Lord Hypatios, their attendants and myself.

As soon as Captain Odysseus eased us as close to the shore as was safe and dropped the great stone anchor, therefore, two teams of crewmen jumped down into the shallows and waded ashore. One team set about creating firepits and placing good-sized flat rocks convenient to them to serve as blocks for any butchery that needed to be done. Then they set up the spits with their supports ready for the cooking to begin. These tasks completed, half went off in search of fire wood while the rest turned to setting up a rudimentary camp ready for the tents to arrive and be pitched in place. Latrines were dug next, a good way down the beach; designed to drain into the sea and be washed out at high tide. Our crew would have left it at that as they usually did, but Hypatios' men added a screen of bushes so that their lord could relieve himself in private. The other team vanished into the forest immediately, armed with slings, spears and bows, hunting for something more substantial than fish for supper. Even though we appeared to be alone here, the captain left a harbour watch aboard as the rest of us jumped down and waded ashore. By the time we had set up our camp and the fire-pits were ablaze, the hunters were back. 'We could have brought deer or goats,' said the leader, a massive oarsman called Elpenor. 'There were plenty enough. But they'd take far too long to roast.' The hunters instead unloaded a half-grown fawn, a couple of tender-looking kids and a selection of hares and rabbits, all of which could be butchered, prepared and cooked almost as quickly as the fish. There would be plenty for all, especially as several loaves of bread almost the size of chariot-wheels had been brought ashore with the amphorae of wine.

With the work done, the men began to take their ease, as did the kings and their unexpected guest, however—as though to match the harbour watch aboard his ship—Odysseus detailed a team led by Elpenor to explore the forest as soon as they had eaten. They were to go further afield than the hunters had done, checking for anyone likely to creep up on us. A gesture from Hypatios assigned his men to join Odysseus' team. 'Though I have to say,' the captain assured Nestor and Hypatios apparently missing the Phthian lord's signal, 'I'm probably being over-cautious.'

'This must be what you hope the beach at Troy will be like,' observed Hypatios by way of reply. 'Comfortable camp, good food, wine; no real need for sizeable patrols…'

'It's not very likely that Priam, his sons, their army and their allies will allow us much peace or comfort,' answered Odysseus easily. 'No matter what sized patrols we send out.'

'But surely it is High King Agamemnon's plan to take such a massive army with him that the Trojans will simply cower behind their walls while he takes his time about besieging and destroying them. Maybe get his troops battle-ready by sacking a few of the lesser local cities. Get supplies and finances that way as well, rather than using up his own great wealth. No particular hurry.'

'Oh, I don't think he's planning on taking much time,' said Odysseus. 'What does King Peleus think?'

'Agamemnon's planning on having the whole matter settled in months, just as I advised,' interrupted Nestor, apparently oblivious to the fact that he had given Hypatios liberty to consider his answer to Odysseus' carefully-timed question.

'He'll need a really impressive force to pull that off,' said Hypatios, sceptically, answering Nestor rather than Odysseus; seeming to challenge the elderly king's advice.

'He has one!' snapped Nestor. 'Twenty Achaean kings have answered his call so far with more ready to join! He's planning to fill a thousand ships before the full force sails.'

ii

'A thousand ships full of the self-styled kings of tiny islands and miniscule kingdoms with their so-called armies! Half of them hoping for enough loot when they sack the city to keep them firmly on their thrones,' observed Hypatios. 'The other half scared of making Agamemnon their enemy and giving him an excuse to attack them next. It's all about self-preservation in the end!'

'Of course it's not,' huffed Nestor. 'It's about the honour of Achaea! We can't allow some eastern princeling to kidnap the wife of an Achaean king and spirit her away to his harem. Why, if we did, none of our wives would be safe!'

'Oh, I don't know,' said Odysseus. 'I can think of a good number of wives who would be perfectly safe. But I believe Lord Hypatios' assessment is accurate enough – except for the fact that many of the worthy and powerful kings involved are not only nervous of making Agamemnon their enemy but *also* hopeful of carrying home a fortune in Trojan loot and a couple of ship-fulls of slaves, preferably from Priam's harem. Sufficient to make their dynasties unassailable—in terms of both finance and succession. Especially with the High King and his heirs as their close friends and allies. Is that how King Peleus sees it, Lord Hypatios?'

'Twenty kings,' said Hypatios dismissively, looking at Nestor. 'Filling a thousand ships with their men. It beggars belief, your majesties.'

'More than twenty kings and princes—or their generals if the kings are too old to join in person,' confirmed Odysseus reclaiming his attention then abruptly changing tack once more. 'Though the precise numbers of soldiers and troop ships have yet to be determined. Did Ajax not tell you all about Agamemnon's plans when he was in Phthia last week?'

'Was it so obvious that he had visited us?' asked Hypatios a little crestfallen. 'The king and the queen wanted his visit kept secret.'

'No doubt for excellent reasons of their own,' nodded Odysseus. 'But yes, I'm afraid it was obvious he had called in. But never mind. Didn't he discuss with King Peleus and his council the nature of the force the High King is assembling?'

'No. He was solely focused on finding his cousin Achilles. Once King Peleus and Queen Thetis convinced him that Achilles had left the court and no-one knew where he and Patroclus had gone, he just decided to move on—he enjoyed the military display first, just as you did, and promised to report to the High King that the Phthian army is in every regard a match for the Myrmidons. He seemed quite limited, frankly; not very flexible.'

'Ajax' strengths are muscular rather than mental,' agreed Odysseus. 'Where did he plan to go to next? Do you know?'

'He had a kind of a list in mind that the High King had apparently talked over with him before sending him on his mission. After Phthia he was off to Skyros, or so he said.'

'Perhaps we'll catch up with him there,' said Odysseus. 'He's always been a bad sailor and a slow traveller. I'd be surprised if King Peleus' mission didn't overtake him. Or Queen Thetis for that matter—did you say that she had gone to Skyros too?' As Odysseus asked this seemingly innocent question, the cooks began to distribute the dinner. The first course was fish served on big fleshy leaves gathered from the undergrowth at the edge of the forest and eaten with our fingers.

'I don't believe the king said the queen had gone to Skyros,' said Hypatios guardedly round a mouthful of mullet. 'I'd guess that if she has even the faintest idea where Achilles might be then she's probably gone in search of him. North to Mount Pelion on the off-chance he is with his old tutor Chiron. Mount Pelion is near the coast: ship is the quickest way to get there—and the most comfortable.'

'Ah,' said Odysseus. 'I must have misunderstood. But neither the king nor the queen actually has any real idea where their son and his companion are. Is that the situation?'

Hypatios shook his head with every appearance of ignorance and regret. 'Achilles and Patroclus often vanish for weeks at a time,' he admitted ruefully. 'Nobody has any real idea of where they go.'

'Returning to Mount Pelion and Chiron for more advanced training in soldiering, hunting and healing does seem to be likely, especially if the young prince has got wind of Agamemnon's plans.' Odysseus, nodded as though that question at least was settled. A flicker went over the Phthian lord's aristocratic face but I could not read any meaning into it. 'Though he does seem to have chosen the most inconvenient time to disappear,' concluded the captain, his tone so bland that it seemed clear to me that his suspicions had been aroused. 'Still, as we're bound south for Skyros ourselves now, I think we'll only head north for Mount Pelion if we find no news there.'

***

Our attention was called away at that moment as the most succulent sections of the kids and young deer arrived on a shield lined with more of the forest's undergrowth, walled with chunks of coarse bread, steaming and smoking like a citadel ablaze. The three aristocrats pulled out their daggers and fell-to. I moved nearer to the fire and grabbed the carcass of a lean hare which I could tear with my bare hands and eat off the bone. I could no longer hear the kings' conversation over the roaring of the fire and the noise the crew was making as they ate and gossiped. But I was able to observe the captain's patrol get up, wiping their hands, and head off into the shadows along the beach, followed by Lord Hypatios' men. Unusually for me I accepted a goblet of wine with which to wash down my meal. It was probably lucky I had done so, because it cleared my throat if not my head; and it was a matter of only a few moments later that Nestor was calling for a song. I had brought my lyre with me and managed to keep it dry as I waded ashore. So I used the sand to get the fat off my fingers, cleared my throat and did my best to oblige.

'*An enemy now delights in the shield I threw away in my haste to retreat. I left it near a bush on the battlefield. It was perfectly good and protected me well. But at least I got myself safely out. Why should I care for my shield after all? Let it go. Some other time I'll find another one just as good." So sang Phobos as he fled, fearful, from the bloody field that his father Ares the God of War had made...*'

'No danger of Nestor interrupting that one,' said Odysseus quietly as I finished. 'He doesn't consort with cowards. He'd rather die than retreat and only associates with like-minded people. It's amazing he's managed to survive for as long has he has, now I come to think of it. Come along. I have to set the guards to keep watch for the night, especially as my patrol hasn't reported back yet; and I could use some company.'

He fell into a pensive silence for a while and gave me time to look around as best I could. There was a full moon on the rise and the beach at least was bright and clear. The forest was something else, though, clothing the nearby hillsides like the bristles on the shoulders of a great black boar. The boar, I thought idly, like the one which had given my captain that great scar up the outside of his left thigh.

'It's not very likely that any locals could assemble a force large enough to attack us by day or while we're awake around the fires,' he said, breaking into my thoughts as we walked the camp's perimeter. 'They'd need a hundred men or so to give us any serious trouble. But once we're asleep, a far smaller force could do a great deal of damage, so we have to be careful.'

'And we'll need to be careful of Lord Hypatios and his men,' I said. 'I don't trust him and they look worryingly murderous.'

'Well observed,' he chuckled. 'Though I suspect that if Hypatios had any real designs on our lives he'd have brought murderers who looked less like murderers.'

'How could a murderer look less like a murderer? He is what he is!'

'That is what King Nestor would say. However, I believe that in some cases, and the most successful I suspect, the murderer is *not* what he appears to be. Don't frown at me; I know it's a new way of thinking for you. But allow me to elucidate. It seems to me that a murderer who looks like a murderer is at a disadvantage compared to a murder who looks like an innocent, harmless man.'

'Would the gods permit such a creature to exist?' I wondered.

'Manifestly. The world is full of men and women who look like the essence of goodness while actually being the distillation of evil. You must never judge a man by his appearance. It is like the old stories of the gods. They are forever disguising themselves. Consider Leda. She thought she was embracing a swan but the swan was really Zeus in disguise having his avian way with her. And let's not even think about poor Europa and her rampant bull! If the gods can mask their true nature when the desire takes them, so can we mortals, surely.'

Our discussion ended there as the patrol returned. 'All well Elpenor?' Odysseus asked.

'No, Captain,' said their leader. 'There's nothing that poses an immediate threat, but there is something I want to show you before we set sail in the morning.'

'And that would be…?' wondered Odysseus.

'Another dead body.'

iii

Odysseus was up as soon as the sky began to brighten and the birds in the forest started their raucous dawn chorus. I woke as soon as he did. I crawled out of the tent I was sharing with Elpenor and a couple of other oarsmen and looked around. I had to steady the pounding of my heart—made worse by a sleepless night—by concentrating on my surroundings rather than on the prospect of viewing yet another mysterious corpse. It was obviously going to be a clear day. There were no clouds visible. If there was a north or north-westerly wind blowing it was not yet obvious to us in the wind-shadow of the hills and headlands to the north and west of us. The sun was also hidden behind the forested heights to the east of us. It seemed apt enough, given our mission, that we should be in the chilly shadow of the craggy island that had seemed so safe a haven last evening in the gentle warmth of that golden sunset.

As the rest of the camp was beginning to stir, Captain Odysseus, Elpenor and I set off along the icy beach towards the low southern headland which separated us from the outer bay. We had been walking silently for only a few minutes before Lord Hypatios and his attendants joined us. No-one seemed keen to talk so we marched silently round the curve of the bay as the day brightened, the sky began to attain the lightest blue colour, like the shell of a duck's egg—or a swan's. A cool wind gusted occasionally making the nearby leaves stir and whisper. The sand stayed cold and clammy, clinging to our feet like slime. After a while we came to the headland and climbed up off the beach onto a low slope with a clear path leading through the woodland to the outer bay. It wasn't much of a climb. We soon reached the crest and began to clamber down. 'This must have been tricky in the dark,' said Odysseus.

'We managed, Captain,' said our guide. He gestured upwards. There was a wide gap in the foliage above our heads. 'Full moon,' he said. 'We didn't even need torches. Besides, torches would have given us away if there had been any enemies out there.'

'So you didn't get a close look at the dead man then?'

'Close enough, Captain. We didn't think it was worth you coming out to look at it in the dark and torches would have given you away just as they would have given us away.'

'So you suspected a trap?' asked Hypatios suddenly.

'Hard to tell. You don't come across a corpse every night on patrol. Could have been anything.'

'You were probably wise,' answered Hypatios.

The conversation was enough to take us down the slope and onto the beach of the outer bay. As soon as we stepped down onto the sand, Odysseus slowed, his eyes narrow. 'Hmmmm,' he said.

It was clear even to me that at least one vessel had overnighted here some days ago. There were fire pits, rocky butcher blocks thick with congealed blood. Bones and offal in two untidy piles lay scattered across the sand. The weather had been as clement here as it had been in Aulis and Phthia—mostly sun and wind: no rain. The outlines of a camp were still visible. Latrines had been dug and used but not filled in. As with ours, there was a section screened off to allow some privacy. Like the scattered offal and the butcher blocks, the latrines were thick with flies even this early on a cool morning. Footsteps led from the campsite to the latrines and to the water's edge in such numbers that the sand was beaten hard. Only one set led across the back of the site to the inland edge of the beach where the undergrowth arched over it like a great green wave waiting to break. We followed these slowly, Odysseus still looking right and left with rapt attention. 'The body is obviously hidden...'

'We think it was buried, though the grave was shallow. Dug by someone either weak or in a hurry—or maybe both.'

'...so what attracted you to it in the dark?'

'A couple of wild dogs. They were quarrelling over it and making a great deal of noise. We didn't know what it was at first. When we went to investigate, we found the dogs tugging at it.'

Odysseus stopped at the spot that the double line of the patrol's approaching and retreating footsteps stopped in a rough semi-circle and he looked around. The smell and the buzzing told us that the corpse was nearby but the captain clearly wanted to assess its surroundings before he came to grips with the carcass itself.

Elpenor interrupted his captain's thoughts. 'It was out on the sand just here,' he said. 'Head and shoulders clear of the bushes, feet still in the undergrowth where the actual grave is. If you can call it a grave. The dogs must have pulled it back in after we left.'

'I see,' said Odysseus. But none of you went down to the water's edge? You all gathered round the corpse, examined it as best you could in the moonlight and came back to report to me and to Lord Hypatios?'

'Yes, Captain.'

'Right. Let's have a look, then.'

We all gathered round and pulled the bushes back to reveal the corpse of a young man lying on its back, wide eyes filled with sand, staring at the sky. The mouth gaped, apparently in shock, also packed with sand, the lower jaw not quite low enough for the beardless chin to cover the great gaping wound where the throat had been cut. Unlike the corpse of Dion the rhapsode, this one was covered in blood. The front of a sturdy tunic was black with it beneath a carapace of ants and flies almost thick enough to pass for a Myrmidon's breastplate. The dogs that had been tugging the corpse about had left deep toothmarks on both arms and started eating the forearm of the right, but other than that they had not done any serious damage. The face at least seemed untouched. As I strove to take it all in, I was shouldered aside. Lord Hypatios crouched over the corpse for an instant and then straightened slowly. 'I know this boy,' he said.

'Really?' asked Odysseus in surprise. 'Who is he?'

'The apprentice! He's Dion the rhapsode's apprentice!'

***

'The murdered rhapsode had an apprentice? And no-one thought to mention the fact?' said Odysseus incredulously.

'Of course not!' snapped Hypatios. 'A mere apprentice! A boy of no account! Why should anyone mention someone of absolutely no importance like an apprentice rhapsode?' His haughty gaze rested on me for an instant and I felt my cheeks flame.

'Well, someone thought he was important!' Odysseus snapped back. 'Important enough to murder at any rate!'

There was a thunderous silence. I was fearful of breaking it and calling the wrath of either or both down on my head. But I had to know. 'Do you think that whoever murdered Dion murdered his apprentice as well?' I quavered.

'I would guess so,' answered Odysseus more calmly. 'At first glance it would seem that any other explanation is stretching coincidence past its natural limits.' He sighed. 'But "guess" is a word I abhor. Let's see whether we can find more clues both here, at the campsite and on the body itself shall we? Then perhaps we can at least move from "I guess" to "I suppose" in the faint hope we will ever get as far as "logic suggests" and "these facts prove"...'

'All this fuss over a no-account boy,' sneered Hypatios.

'It may be, my Lord,' grated Odysseus, 'that his true importance lies not in himself but in what he can tell us of larger and more dangerous matters. If you do not wish to wait, I won't detain you but I would ask you to warn King Nestor that we will not be setting sail for a little while yet.'

'As you wish,' sniffed Hypatios. 'As long as we leave in time to reach Skyros before nightfall!'

I watched the Phthian lord stalk back across the beach with his attendants close behind. My captain did not—he had already returned to his examination of the dead boy and his surroundings. As he looked down, he suddenly started speaking in a low voice. 'Pay no attention to Lord Hypatios,' he said. 'You will meet many such men and you should take no notice at all of their pride and prejudice.'

'Don't worry, Captain,' I replied. 'I am the son of a powerful trading house as well as an apprentice rhapsode. I can stand on that—it is firm ground.'

Odysseus glanced up. 'Meaning?' he asked.

'The cloak Lord Hypatios is wearing if of Cretan or Trojan wool, imported to Aulis for weaving and dying. His tunic is Egyptian linen imported from Alexandria ready coloured, figured and embroidered; that is how I can tell it from more local cloth from Pylos, the Pyloan flax that makes the ropes and sails on your ship, Captain, and also underpins the riches that support King Nestor. His belt and footwear were both made in Naxos from local leather and, once again, imported to the markets on the mainland by vessels such as my father's. The dagger he carries is made of bronze imported as brass and tin via Troy and made by our metalworkers in Chalcis then honed on one of our whetstones. Were it not for men of no account such as me and my family, he would be walking barefoot, naked and defenceless.'

Odysseus paused, still looking at me with the slightest of frowns. Then he smiled. 'Remind me never to underestimate you or your family,' he said. Then the smile vanished and he turned to the dead boy. 'We're going to have to carry the poor lad back aboard so I can examine him properly,' he said. 'I can take my time with that. But this is my one and only chance to examine the beach and I suspect that neither Nestor nor Hypatios will be willing to wait too long. So…' He let the bush fall back then he stood and looked down the beach at the set of tracks leading up from the confusion of footprints at the water's edge. 'Look,' he said, either to me or to Elpenor his crew-man. 'These footprints suggest that one man walked up here but three men walked back. Now there's a puzzle.'

I looked at the footprints he was describing and it was clear that he was correct. The sand was solid enough to show the shapes of the prints quite clearly. One set with the toe pointing up towards the bush we were standing beside, three sets with the toes pointing down towards the water's edge. Some of them overlapped each-other of course, but the overall pattern was quite clear. My mind whirled, seeking an explanation for the strange phenomenon.

But Odysseus continued to talk. 'However, note how some footprints are deeper than others. And see, this set with the toe facing seawards has particularly deep toe and heel-marks, with a little sand kicked up behind them every now and then. Now what does that tell us?'

iv

It told me nothing at all. I looked at Elpenor a little desperately but he just shrugged. Fortunately, the captain did not hesitate to enlighten us. 'Two men, one walking backwards, carrying something heavy but motionless between them to this very place and then two men, unencumbered walking side by side back down to the sea. Which tells us something else of importance at once—namely that the murder was done there and only the burial was done here. Something that the absence of blood on the surrounding bushes and ground had already suggested. I have cut enough throats on the battlefield to know how much blood gets sprayed everywhere immediately after the act. So, two men carried the dead body and probably some kind of a shovel up here, dug the makeshift grave behind this bush, buried the corpse, then walked back down to the water once more. But wait.' He stepped onto the sand beside the tracks, lifted his foot and compared the sizes. 'Two small men—almost boys, if the size of their feet is a guide. And not all that strong if the depth of the grave is anything to go by.'

Frowning with concentration and stooping so as not to miss the smallest detail, Odysseus led us down alongside that set of footprints until they became lost in the crowd which flattened the sand to the tideline. He paused here, looking from right to left. On his right, the deserted camp-site; on his left a little distance away, the latrines. He hesitated, deep in thought. He turned left, frowning, but did not yet step forward. 'Too good just to drop their loincloths, hold up their tunics and wade into the water to relieve themselves,' he said. 'As are we, for we have kings and lords aboard and to be fair the water is icy at night while, at our anchorage, the slope of the seabed is steep, rocky and dangerous, unlike this beach. And someone was too modest to use the latrine under public view. As is Lord Hypatios. Interesting. Deserving of a closer look.'

The latrines were a trench walled to knee-hight on this side by the sand dug out to make them. The inland section, perhaps a quarter of the whole length, was further protected by a screen of bushes that had clearly been cut from the undergrowth and then erected, using the low wall of sand to hold them firm. The path from the camp to the facility, beaten flat by the number of feet that had followed it, arched round the inland end of this as the other end was of course open to the sea. Abruptly and with no warning, Odysseus was following this path. He rounded the inland end of the latrine and stopped, looking down. Several tides had done their work and almost everything had been washed away. He squatted and for a moment I thought he might be going to avail himself of the facility. But no; he swung round, duck-like, his gaze raking everything nearby—beach, trench, fly-covered effluent, low sand wall, bushes… 'Ah,' he said. 'I think we have our killing ground.' He gestured. On the far lip of the trench, on the sand wall and on the bushes above it was a spray of dark splotches, seething with flies. 'Caught here at his most defenceless. Surprised by one attacker, perhaps two, though I would guess a strong child could have done the work unaided, were his dagger sharp enough. Throat cut guaranteeing silence, seclusion having already been provided. Guaranteeing silence, but also releasing that first spray of blood before the rest ran down his chest. As, no doubt, he toppled backwards and clutched his hands over the wound, trying to stanch the flow. Fruitlessly, of course. There might have been blood on the sand beneath our feet but it has been disturbed, so that all trace has gone. He would have been dead in a dozen heartbeats or so. Then two slight, almost boyish, men carried him up the beach, almost as soon as he was dead, I'd guess.' He grimaced at the word. 'But, until the flies came, it would be a sharp-eyed man who would notice the blood on the sand and the bushes as easily as we did.' He straightened up and carried on. 'Let's look at the rest of the scene of this crime, shall we?'

A clear difference between here and the inner bay was immediately obvious as we came out from the latrines to look more closely at the main camp site. Whereas that beach, narrow though it was, seemed clean, here there was another low wall—this time made of sea-wrack, mostly of green weed, going grey as it died, liberally mixed with fronds and branches of brown. The sea-facing side of the foot-flattened area had been partially cleared of this—the dry bits no doubt added to the kindling in the fire-pits that pocked this area. While I was counting these pits and trying to assess how many they would have fed—quite a number going by the piles of scattered bones—Odysseus was giving closer attention to the weed itself. 'Two,' he decided after a while, straightening and looking out to sea.

'Two what, Captain?' asked his bemused crew-man.

Odysseus pointed. The weed had two marked gullies in it, with trenches coming through them deep enough for the water to be pushing foamy fingers further inland, the same as it was in the latrine. 'Two ships, run up onto the sand almost side by side. Overnighting here together. Not so long ago either, judging by how little in fact the piles of bones and offal have been scattered by the local carrion eaters, not to mention how well-preserved the boy's body is, despite dogs, carrion birds, ants and flies. At least a hundred people were fed and watered here, judging by those bones and the number of fire-pits. Either just before or just after Dion's murder by the look of things. After, I'd surmise, given the position the ship would have needed to be in for his body to get swept past Euboea Island and under our bows. But, either way, one of the vessels beached here was certainly the ship Dion was murdered on.'

'But how can you know that, Captain?' I asked, scarcely able to believe the speed of his deduction or the certainty in his voice.

'Logic, boy; logic. What ship would this unfortunate apprentice be travelling aboard other than the one that carried his master?'

***

Elpenor, who had led Odysseus' patrol last night and who accompanied us now was one of the most powerful oarsmen aboard. He had, therefore, enormous strength and impressively wide shoulders. He was also a battle-hardened warrior, fearful neither of death nor dead men. When Odysseus was finished his examination of the beach, he had no compunction whatsoever at brushing the ants and flies off the front of the dead boy's tunic, as Odysseus took one more look at it in the place where we had found the body. Although one arm had been partially consumed, it was easy to see that from wrist to elbow, both had been covered with blood. And, when Odysseus opened the loosely clenched fists, the fingers and palms were almost as thick with it as the front of the poor boy's tunic. The captain continued his swift examination, revealing nothing more than the corpse's tunic-skirts, his pitifully thin legs which seemed hardly strong enough to bear the body—let alone allow the boy to walk—and his cheap leather sandals. He nodded. 'That's all I need to see here, Elpenor,' he said. 'You can take him now.'

Lifting the corpse over his shoulder, Elpenor straightened. Holding the stick-legs gently against his chest while the staring head and half-eaten arms hung down his back, sluggishly dribbling sand, he started walking back to the inner beach. Thus the four of us returned to Odysseus' ship and the impatient men waiting to set sail for Skyros.

As we walked, we talked. Or, at least I did; to begin with. ''So, can I get things straight in my head?' I said to the captain.

'By *things* you mean the sequence of events leading to the apprentice rhapsode's murder?'

'Yes.'

'I can understand why you would want to do that as a matter of some urgency, especially in case the man who slaughters rhapsodes and their apprentices so brutally is waiting for us on Skyros, which I must admit seems quite likely.'

'So,' I persisted, talking to overcome my growing nervousness. 'To begin at what seems to be the beginning, King Priam of Troy sent an embassy to King Menelaus of Sparta. That embassy included Prince Paris, no doubt amongst many other Trojan nobles, merchants and businessmen. But when the embassy left, they took Menelaus' wife Helen with them either eloping or as the victim of kidnap. This was a particularly wounding blow on at least two levels. First, Menelaus is King Agamemnon's brother and the insult to the King of Sparta also reflected on the High King of Mycenae, whose power is great and whose honour cannot be damaged without the direst of consequences. Secondly, and on a more personal level, perhaps, Achaean kings only take one wife and, unless she dies, she is the mother of the next generation of kings. Menelaus, therefore, stands not only wifeless but childless, facing the dangerous prospect of his royal line dying out when he dies. While Helen may simply join Prince Paris' harem, on which he will, like his father, sire as many as fifty sons in due time.'

'I haven't heard it put like that,' said Odysseus. 'You certainly do not make it sound like the stuff of legend, suitable for one of your songs!'

'But,' I continued, 'High King Agamemnon, for a range of political and financial reasons, which my father explained to me just before I joined your crew, has chosen to make the kidnap or elopement of his sister in law an excuse for war. He sends emissaries such as Prince Ajax, King Nestor and yourself not only to Troy to negotiate Queen Helen's return, but also to threaten and bribe all the Achaean kings into joining him in a great war to rescue her. He and Nestor—amongst others I suspect—envision a short but immensely profitable campaign that will seal their fame, fill their treasuries and settle their dynasties for generations to come, as well as giving the Achaeans a major foothold in Asia beyond the little settlements that dot the coast of Anatolia now. Others, including Peleus, Lycomedes and yourself, fear a campaign lasting for years rather than months while doing untold damage to your leaderless and increasingly impoverished kingdoms at home. And at the heart of this stand Prince Achilles and his Myrmidons, their importance symbolic as much as practical, but nevertheless incalculable. If they join the High King, even the waverers will follow. If they refuse, his grand project may very likely collapse, his standing, honour and power damaged beyond recall.'

'You have clearly thought this through,' said Odysseus. 'I'm impressed. Can you take your reasoning further still?'

'Surely it all turns on the absence of Achilles. An absence that in itself gives nothing whatever away. Is he hiding because he is fearful of being made to take the Myrmidons into a war he does not wish to fight? Or is he secretly training to prepare himself to stand at the head of his army as the greatest warrior of his generation?'

'Is he, in fact, doing what his mother says—or is he doing what his father says?' Odysseus mused.

'Each one of his parents believes the other to be wrong,' I continued. 'The only thing they seem to agree on is that they have no idea where he and his companion Patroclus actually are. So Queen Thetis has gone north to Mount Pelion to stop him training if that is what he's doing, while King Peleus is sending messages south to Skyros, no doubt seeking King Lycomedes' advice and support. Because King Peleus finds himself in a strange position. He believes his son wishes to lead his Myrmidons at Agamemnon's side but he fears that if he supports him in this aim, he will make an implacable enemy of his wife Queen Thetis, his kingdom will wither into beggary long before any loot comes home, and his dynasty will die with his only son beneath the indestructible walls of Troy.'

'And in the midst of this,' said Odysseus 'we have someone so desperate to stop Peleus passing on his fears to Lycomedes that they have murdered not only the messenger but the messenger's apprentice. It's no wonder that you're thinking things through so carefully, lad, because there's a fair chance that if Lord Hypatios as replacement message-bearer isn't the murderer's next target, then there's a fair chance that you are.'

v

We waited on the beach beside *Thalassa* while Odysseus, unusually, hesitated. He began to discuss the quandary in which he found himself in low, pensive tones. He was really talking to himself but I reacted as though he was still talking to me. 'We have moved the body. There was no further information to be gleaned from the grave itself and carrying the poor lad here has probably disturbed any further information that might have been on the corpse itself. But do we dare wash it? If we rinse it off here and now what else might we lose? But if we take it aboard as it is, we still have the option of washing it later.'

'I'd suggest we take it aboard as it is then, Captain' I said quietly. 'That way you can continue to examine it sooner and wash it later.'

He nodded. 'You might be right or you might be wrong. But at least we reached the decision through reasoning,' he said. He shouted a series of orders. A couple of oarsmen appeared on the foredeck just above us. They leaned down over the side and we handed the body up to them. But that's where things went wrong. The corpse was limp and disturbingly heavy. The sand it was covered with made it hard to hold. The men on deck seemed to take a firm grip of the chest, their hands under the flaccid arms, but an instant later it was falling. The heavy ball of its head smacked Elpenor in the face and he reeled back, stunned. He collided with Odysseus and both staggered away as the wave, generated by the corpse falling into the water, washed towards them. I didn't even think. My body was in action long before my consciousness caught up. I dived forward and wrapped myself around the boy as though we were wrestling. His dead weight pulled me down with him as his limp arms wrapped themselves around me in reply to my grip. By the time I fully realised what I had got myself into, I discovered that I was clutching the still chest in a tight hug. His knees, as loosely active as his arms, battered me painfully in the pit of my stomach as though he had come to life and was fighting me off. His feet kicked me on the shins, both together as though somehow linked. My face was jammed unsettlingly close to the gape of his throat. As the water washed through it, scouring the sand away, the great wound opened and closed like the mouth of some huge fish. The severed tubes washed in and out like the fish's tongue. It seemed to me that they must have somehow been torn loose to be waving about like that, but of course I knew nothing about the inner workings of the throat so this was just an impression. My grip on his chest tightened convulsively and a cloud of bubbles burst out of one of the sundered tubes, brushing over my face like the touch of a leper, making me jerk my own head back and shout with shock, losing what little air was still in my lungs.

I had just reached this point in my dazed half-dream, with the shock of it all beginning to pull me towards reality, when reality caught up with me. Several fists closed on the back of my tunic. My companion and I were dragged unceremoniously to the surface. Only when my face came out of the water did I realise that I was almost completely out of breath. I took one huge, shuddering gasp. 'That was quick thinking, lad,' said Odysseus as he set me on my feet while his Elpenor reclaimed the corpse.

'I didn't think at all, Captain,' I wheezed.

'Thinking or not thinking, you stopped him escaping. Well done.'

As we were speaking, Elpenor handed the now-washed corpse up once more and this time the dripping body made it safely aboard. Then the pair of them handed me up as well. The captain came next—unaided—and by the time the big oarsman jumped over the bulwark, the sail-handlers had raised the anchor and we were off. The dead boy lay, alone and forlorn on the foredeck as Odysseus ran lightly back to the stern where the helmsman, and his assistants kept tight hold of the steering board, while the oarsmen eased us round until we were facing out of the bay. Then, at a gesture from Odysseus the rowing master dictated the rhythm, the oarsmen took up the chorus and the ship headed straight for open water.

As we came past the mouth of the outer bay I looked across at the camp-site we had spent much of the morning so far examining but it was too distant for me to make out any details so the place added nothing more to our store of knowledge. It did prompt me, however, to turn back for a closer look at the boy on the deck. I walked over to him, dripping, until I could see him quite clearly. He lay on his back, eyes and mouth wide, the black-blood still set on the front of his tunic, despite the soaking; though quite a lot seemed to have been washed off his arms and half-open hands. The last of the sand with which he had been covered was beginning to stir as the heat of the morning sun dried it sufficiently to set the sand-hoppers that had survived their swim to jumping and calling the last remaining ants out into the light. They mostly came out of his thick, matted hair, crawling up onto his face. Some came from folds in his tunic, scurrying back onto that Myrmidon-black section on top of his chest. I watched them in a kind of dream, revolted yet fascinated at the same time. The wide eyes looked more human now that the sand had been washed out of them. The expression on the dead face frozen into shock and horror. It was only after several moments that I realised his loincloth had somehow fallen round his ankles—which at least explained how he had managed to kick me with both feet at once.

I was still staring, sickened but entranced, when the captain arrived at my side with a pair of sail handlers in tow. 'Now,' he said, 'let's see what more this poor boy can tell us.'

***

He ordered that the corpse be stripped, then he examined it

minutely, frowning with concentration as the sailhandlers working with him laid out the tunic, loincloth and sandals a little distance away, close to the bulwark to the right of the high, back-curving prow. He probed gently down its back from head to heels. 'No swelling or softness,' he said thoughtfully, as he pushed his finger beneath the thick dark hair. 'He wasn't knocked out, then. He wasn't attacked like you were in Troy.'

I nodded, dumbly. 'No. I see that,' I said as the sail-handlers turned the body onto its back once more. But the front of the body apparently revealed nothing new either.

Odysseus sat back on his heels and began to discuss what he had deduced. The first thing he remarked on was something as far away from that severed throat as it was possible to get. 'His loin cloth was round his ankles when he came aboard,' he said. 'I don't remember that being the case when we slung him over Elpenor' shoulder. It must have come down when he was in the water. Did you notice?'

'Not really, Captain. I was looking at his throat. But he did manage to kick me with both feet at once.'

'It's instructive, though, even if we could have worked it out logically from the facts we already know.'

'What facts, Captain?'

'That he was killed while using the latrine behind the wall of bushes. The blood was on the sand and the bushes there, so he was facing that way when he was attacked. He had eased his loincloth down just enough to allow him to urinate, therefore, and he never had the chance to pull it up again. Had he been defecating, of course, the loincloth would already have been around his ankles and he would have been facing the other way entirely. Somebody approached him. Somebody who presented no immediate threat. They went close enough to reach out and bang!' He clapped his hands. 'The deed is done. His throat is cut, blood sprays across the latrine and onto the screen of bushes. He clutches his wound with both hands as he goes to his knees, blood cascading down his breast. He is pushed back—or topples back—to lie on the sand rather than falling into the latrine itself. He dies, swiftly and silently, most of the blood pouring down his chest soaks into his tunic as he does so.'

'But the killer is not alone,' I took up the story. 'Two people move him up to the undergrowth then or soon after, one walking backwards and the other forward. They bury him in a shallow grave.' I paused, frowning. 'You suggest that they might be smaller and weaker than the average sailor because of the size of the footprints and the shallowness of the grave. But, more importantly, surely, there is another question. There were a hundred people there, maybe more. Why did no-one see any of this happening?'

'There must have been at least two elements,' he said. 'Darkness and distraction.'

'But what could distract so many so completely?'

'I can only think of one thing—a rhapsode.' He paused, calculating. 'So either there were two rhapsodes or the boy died before Dion did.'

'Very well,' I said, 'but even if Dion was singing the most engrossing song, surely it is not so easy to cut a throat so that it can be done in an instant. Surely a hand over his mouth and a blade at his throat would give him the chance to struggle and call out...'

He looked up at me. 'That's how you'd do it? Come up behind him, arm round his chest, hand over his mouth, blade across his throat?'

'That's how they do it on the docks,' I said. My tone told him I knew what I was talking about.

'On the battlefield it's different,' he said. 'The man you're going to kill is usually lying on his back, wounded, incapacitated; dying in agony as often as not. No chance of getting behind him at all. Also, he's covered in armour. Helmet down past his chin, cuirass up to his neck. Maybe a hand's width of throat in between. So you slide your blade in one side—usually his left.' He was close enough to touch the side of my throat with his forefinger. 'The point is often sharper than the edge in any case, so you push it right through and then pull it up towards you. Cuts through the blood vessels and all the tubes there; its effectiveness depending on how sharp the edge actually is. But in my experience it's not too hard to do. Swift and silent.'

'Is that what's been done here?' I asked, imagining how it would have felt had his finger been the point of a sharp bronze dagger.

'It looks like it,' he answered. 'The wound seems wider and deeper on the left side of the throat; it cuts deep into the muscle, see? Little more than the point came out at the right. On the battlefield, the blade would sometimes pull things loose in a way that I suppose wouldn't happen cutting in from the front in the manner you describe, and that's clearly what's happened here.'

He and I looked down at the dead throat. Sharp though it might have been, the fatal dagger had certainly pulled things there loose as it was torn out through the front of the throat. 'Does that get us any farther?' I wondered.

'It allows us to put the actual murder together more accurately and in more detail,' he said. 'The lad has his loincloth down, holding the front of his tunic up as he uses the latrine. One hand on the tunic and one hand on his member if experience is any guide. The murderer walks up beside him. It's dark so he's not sure who it is and neither are we. But something is said that puts his mind at rest for an instant. During which his shadowy companion stabs a dagger into the left side of his throat pushes it right through and jerks it forward. He falls to his knees as the blood spurts. He clutches the wound and topples backwards, his face frozen with shock and horror. He dies within almost no time at all. The body is moved and buried before anyone else notices. By two people who are not much older or bigger than he is. Look at his sandals.' He held one up for me to inspect. 'The same size as the footprints we examined so closely. I assume no-one else has been alerted to these gruesome events, but we will find out when we catch up with the ship that carried the rhapsode Dion, because that was bound for Skyros. As are we. And I think I'd better check on our progress.'

Odysseus rose and turned to stride back to the rear deck. I glanced down at the dead boy then followed him.

When I caught up with him, he was standing beside Nestor, Hypatios and the helmsman. 'Are we still heading west under oars?' he said. 'We've come much further than I'd have thought.'

'We're still seeking the wind,' said Nestor.

'Skiathos,' said the helmsman tersely, gesturing to the island that stood to the north west of us. 'It seems to be blocking the northerly we need, Captain. And in any case the wind seems to have swung to westwards.' He wet his finger and held it up. 'Yes,' he said after a moment. 'It's swinging westward. Which will help us go east of south. If we can find it.'

'Well,' said Odysseus, 'if we haven't found it by noon we'll have to run south with the oars.' But even as he spoke, a strange change overcame the motion of the ship. The rhythm of the oars didn't vary, but our speed westward suddenly seemed to get faster—as though Poseidon himself had grasped the hull and was pulling us towards Euboea, or rather towards that channel just north of it. No sooner had the ship began to thrill with this strange new motion than the first puff of the north wind blew onto our cheeks.

'Turn south at once,' ordered Odysseus, his voice tense. 'Row us out of this current before it pulls us too far off course, then set the sail. Trim it to sail east of south.'

The bustle on the rear deck and midships, as the ship swung southward and began to fight clear of the current, while the sail was set and angled at the captain's order, became so great that I soon felt in the way. I went forward, therefore, and stood on the deck at the bow which was empty of everyone else except the dead boy. In my hurry to get to a good vantage point and look away along our new course, I kicked one of his sandals without realising it. It slid across the deck and fell over the side just as the ship began to turn, still under the power of its oars. I watched the sandal almost mindlessly as it bobbed there on the undulating surface, floating away, its departure from the ship's side speeded by our movement round onto that new course. Almost immediately, it was far beyond the ends of the oars themselves, beyond even the spreading disturbance as they churned the water into white foam. The wind strengthened, the sail thundered and filled. The oars came back aboard. *Thalassa* groaned as the yards, mast and rigging took the strain. It shuddered, then began to move deliberately out of the grip of that strange current and gathered speed as it settled onto the southward reach. All the time I leaned on the forward bulwark watching that lone sandal sailing away from us. It seemed to be moving with a purpose of its own, as though it had decided that, wherever we were bound for, it was going back to Phthia.

I stood there, alone and lost in thought until, with a suddenness that shocked the breath out of me, Lord Hypatios grabbed my shoulder from behind. 'It's lucky you are of so little account, apprentice rhapsode,' he said, 'or I could have slipped a dagger between your ribs and had you over the side with no-one any the wiser…'

4 – Skyros

i

The harbour at Skyros turned out to be the most welcoming of all. It was a relief to get there at the end of a disturbingly long afternoon trapped aboard Odysseus' ship with Lord Hypatios, his grim-looking servants, and his threats. It was fortunate that we had caught the steady breeze as early as we did, for even under full sail it took from mid-morning to early evening to get there. I spent as much time as possible close to the captain and well away from the Phthian lord and his sinister cohorts. So, almost by accident, I got a fine chance to admire the Odysseus' ship-handling skills. These were superior to those of any captain aboard any of my father's fleet and second only to his ability to apply logic to apparently insoluble mysteries. But of course Odysseus was a fighting captain, not a trader and his vessel *Thalassa* was a lean, dangerous warship not a fat-sided merchantman.

As we approached the tiny islet of Skiropula in mid-afternoon, Odysseus ordered that the sailhandlers trim the great rectangular linen sail so that the steady north-westerly could push us a point or two further eastwards. Nestor and the helmsman looked askance at him because trimming the sail much further risked losing the wind altogether, but the captain knew his ship and *Thalassa* settled onto her new course sailing across the wind without complaint. I noticed Nestor breathing a sigh of relief: the linen that the sail was made of came from his slave-run flax beds and linen-weaving workshops in Pylos; he would have taken its failure to hold the wind personally. As it was, the cliff-walled mound of rock passed close on our right beam just as the northern headland of Skyros loomed more distantly south-east on our left. Late afternoon found us to the east of the even smaller islet of Skirou with the northern promontory of Skyros still on our left, but closer now. As evening approached, we sailed closer and closer to Skyros' rocky and forbidding coast. At last Odysseus ordered that we furl the sail. Under oars, he guided us carefully through a narrow, rock-fanged channel between two desolate headlands that started Nestor talking of the clashing rocks again. Close on our right lay the northern point of Valaxa, the hilly finger of island that protects the haven at Skyros. On our left, seemingly just beyond the blades of our oars, the tip of a promontory jutting out from the larger island itself. Beneath our hull a ridge of rock that joined the two and raised the stony sea-bed dangerously close. Once through, we turned left once more to head back north-eastward. Powering forward at full-speed it still took us nearly an hour to reach the island's main harbour. The sun had slipped behind the heights of Valaxa, and the western jut of Skyros which was so nearly joined to it. The anchorage was in shadow, therefore, but all the way along our final approach we had seen bludgeoning brightness beating down on the city dead ahead and the citadel sitting squarely on top of it.

The city of Skyros faced south-west and was shaped like a gigantic arrow-head pointing at the sky, its bearing and form dictated by its unique situation. Its houses, squares, temples and public buildings mounted a steep hillside. Wide and welcoming at the foot of the hill, lining the curve of the beach and the anchorage seaward of it, they were piled one on top of the other as they rose seemingly vertically. The width of the city grew narrower and narrower as the hill itself came to a point like the fang of an enormous wolf. And there, right at the very top, seated on the pinnacle of the mountainous metropolis, sat Lycomedes' citadel. Although we were in cool evening shadows as we approached our anchorage below, the citadel still burned brightly in the last of the sun, as though the home of the gods had somehow come down into the real world.

Straight ahead, beneath this stunningly impressive hillside, a low, flat valley stretched away into the distance. It was a fertile area, well watered and full of farms that supplied the city and the citadel above it. It remained more sparsely populated than the city itself, however, because it was effectively defenceless against sea-raiders. This was a situation compounded, I knew, because the island of Skyros was constructed like a giant hornet:

precipitous hills made the northern and southern sections wide as well as high, and this central wasp-waist section narrow as well as low. There was, as far as I knew, another anchorage at the far side of this but it was hardly ever used—except by marauders from the east creeping in off the sea to pillage and steal whatever they could.

At the main anchorage, however, there was a jetty reaching out into the bay with one ship tied to it already while the beach was littered with fishing boats and fishermen mending their nets. Odysseus took us along the opposite side of the jetty to the other large vessel and we shipped oars and tied up there. A brief discussion between Hypatios and Nestor never really became confrontational but in the end one representative from each man's band of followers went running up the hill to tell King Lycomedes—who had no doubt been warned of the ship's approach long ago—precisely who had come to visit him so that he could prepare a suitable welcome. Then we disembarked more slowly.

***

The wise Odysseus had sent no-one to proclaim his arrival, though he sent his chief oarsman Elpenor to the harbourmaster to announce his vessel's presence, discuss port fees and enquire as to what other shipping had passed through recently. As we waited for the massive oarsman's return, and the sailhandlers carried the apprentice rhapsode's corpse below-deck, the captain leaned against the bulwark beside the back-curving prow and expressed his surprise. 'I had rather taken it for granted,' he said, 'that the two ships which ran ashore on Skopelos would have arrived here before we did. They must have been days ahead of us.'

'Perhaps that's one of them,' I said, gesturing at the ship on the far side of the jetty.

'No,' he answered. 'I know it. It's named *Nerites* and it's neither of the ones we were expecting to find here. Looks as though we may have to wait a little while yet before we can begin to look further into the murders of Dion the rhapsode and his apprentice.'

Elpenor returned with much of the information the captain

required, but as to the question of the ships from Skopelos, he shrugged and shook his head. Odysseus frowned, then, still deep in thought, he went to work. He knew all too well that he would need every man he had at hand to transport everything he and Nestor had brought with them up to Lycomedes' hilltop citadel. That, I assumed, was why he had waited for the strongest of them to return and left the weakest aboard as harbour watch and guards of the dead body.

I found the steep streets so testing that I soon fell behind the captain and his men, Nestor, Hypatios and theirs. For once, my companions were too busy and preoccupied to offer me any help. On more than one occasion I seriously considered giving up and returning to the ship to camp-out with the harbour watch and the apprentice rhapsode's corpse. This was especially the case because every now and then I got the impression that I was being watched. As a stranger, half blind and partially crippled, I was hardly surprised to be drawing the attention of the locals. But this was something different. I soon got the decided impression that, although the scrutiny lingered on me as I puffed along behind my captain and his crew, it was they who were actually being watched. Secretly. Guardedly. But several things goaded me onwards. I naturally wanted to be close to Odysseus, for I was still unnerved by Lord Hypatios' threats. Moreover, it was clear that the captain planned to do more here than give Lycomedes his gifts and pass Agamemnon's messages on, even if that mysterious pair of ships had not yet docked here. And there was the matter of the two signet rings still lying in his purse.

Further, never having visited the place, I was keen to see whether the rumours I had heard about it were true and that the self-indulgent old king had fallen almost completely under the influence of the Asian ways of cities such as Troy. That instead of a single wife, he had a harem like King Priam's; that he had fathered almost as many daughters as Priam had fathered sons, who he kept secreted with his wives, concubines, female servants and slaves in women's quarters which it was death for a man to enter uninvited. That on the rare occasions his women were allowed into masculine society, their beauty was hidden behind veils in the eastern fashion. And, perhaps most temptingly of all, that when the women did come out of their inviolable quarters, it was usually to perform the most exquisite dances dedicated to Eros, the god of passion and procreation. But even given all this motivation, I believe I would never have completed my vertiginous journey had not some kindly townspeople taken pity on me and helped me up the final steep-sloping path leading to my destination. And in so doing, they drove the unsettling impression I had gained further down the hill out of my mind altogether.

King Lycomedes' citadel was an impressive place. Some trick of its positioning made it seem circumscribed and limited by the hilltop plateau on which it sat but nothing could have been further from the truth. True, the finely made walls that towered above the topmost houses of the city limited it on one elevation, though even here the great gate, with a tall, square tower on either side of it, opened to a courtyard so large that anyone who did not know the place would be as astonished by it as I was. The gate towers were duplicated half way round the curve of each wall, giving the inner courtyard a reassuring air of being constantly watched and guarded. Though I was aware that the tall walls, with their stones so massive they must surely be the work of giants or legendary gods, served a more warlike defensive role. Like the valley below, Lycomedes' citadel had been attacked on more than one occasion by Lykian brigands and assorted marauders from Lesbos and the pirate islands east of it. If the citadel of Skyros wasn't on a constant war-footing, then it was on something very like it.

ii

As I entered the huge gates, however, all such thoughts were driven from my mind. The palace within this great wall arched round, making the courtyard into a circle. The main building, with its rear extending the hilltop on which it had been constructed, towered immediately opposite the gates—two wings reached out on either side, deep buildings near the palace coming as far as the towers mid-way to the gates, after which the massive walls were plain and sheer on both sides with a walkway along the top. But although the walls and towers were imposing, they were nothing compared with the palace itself. The whole front of the place was faced with marble so white that it must have come from the quarries on Thasos, and I would hardly have been surprised if Zeus and Hera had come out of it to welcome me.

The heat of that torrid afternoon lingered up here and, together with the breathlessness resulting from my climb, I found myself reeling, dangerously close to fainting as I entered the overwhelming fortification. My disorientation was deepened by the sudden appearance of a guard captain in full bronze armour backed up by a unit of four leather-clad gate keepers. The dazzling captain demanded to know my name and reason for being here. No sooner had I identified myself, however, than his attitude softened. 'Ah, the rhapsode. We've been expecting you,' he said and dismissed his little cohort back to gate duty. 'Follow me please. And if I may say, from the look of you I think it is as well King Lycomedes' own rhapsode will be playing at this evening's feast. Perhaps a night off will allow you to catch your breath. But as I say, the king has been expecting a rhapsode from Phthia, and he will certainly wish to listen to one of your songs in due course. In the mean-time I believe you have been assigned to King Odysseus' immediate entourage and will be housed with them within the palace itself.'

The officer led me through a side entrance into the main building and a blessedly cool shade closed over us at once. As with Peleus' palace in Phthia, this palace was a maze of corridors but, perhaps because I was exhausted and light-headed, I could make no sense of them. I simply followed the polished bronze cuirass as its owner led me deeper and deeper into the place with no idea where I was going or how I would find my way out again. But fortunately there were three familiar faces in the four bed chamber to which he finally delivered me. 'Ah, there you are, lad,' said the broad-shouldered oarsman Elpenor. 'The captain told Perimedes, Eurylocus and me to keep an eye out for you.' He gestured at his two companions as he named them, then continued. 'You look all-in. This is your bed, you'd better sit on it.' I did, gratefully. 'Here,' he continued, 'a drink of water will cheer you up.' He gestured to one of the others and suddenly I was holding a cup of cool water, surprised to discover I had put down my lyre and modest bag of possessions without even realising it. 'You can wash and relieve yourself in the common parts at the end of the corridor,' he continued. 'And we'll get someone to brush that peplos down for you. I don't suppose you have a more respectable himation with you? King Lycomedes likes things formal, especially when he's entertaining kings, princes and assorted lords.'

'Princes?' I asked, my head beginning to clear.

'Oh yes. I thought you'd have worked it out from the fact that his ship is tied up next to ours—the captain says you're pretty sharp-witted. Odysseus and Nestor, of course. And also Ajax, son of King Telamon, Prince of Salamis. Best fighter in Achaea, except for his cousin Prince Achilles, wherever he may be.'

My head was clearing more rapidly now, and the import of the earlier section of our conversation hit me. 'Himation,' I said. 'You asked if I had a himation—which I do not. Does that mean I'm expected to attend the feast of welcome?'

'Of course you are,' chuckled Elpenor. 'I really don't think you understand yet just how important King Odysseus' rhapsode actually is, especially as he's never bothered to employ one before. You're stuck with it, just as you were in King Peleus' court.'

'The guard who brought me here said King Lycomedes was expecting a rhapsode to arrive from Phthia,' I said. 'He must have meant Dion and didn't know he's dead. I think he supposed it was me the King's expecting.' It was, perhaps, a mark of my continued disorientation that I did not see the sinister implications of my words, despite what Captain Odysseus had said earlier about any rhapsode being next on the murderer's list. After King Peleus' new message-bearer Hypatios, that is.

'There you are then,' said Elpenor. 'You'd better get your best song polished up because you'll be singing it sooner or later.'

'King Lycomedes has his own rhapsode,' I said. 'So apparently I won't have to sing tonight.'

'Just as well,' said Elpenor with a shake of his head. 'You don't look as though you could sit up straight for any length of time—let alone sit up and sing!'

***

Like King Peleus, King Lycomedes held his feast of welcome in the great chamber of his megaron. The tables were erected around the edges of the big square room, all equidistant from the circular fire pit in the centre of the ornate, multicoloured floor, much as they had been in Phthia. They were not, however, equidistant from the seat of power. King Lycomedes sat on his throne, raised higher than the places for his honoured guests to right and left, for the senior guests down to common people who stood marginally above the servants but who were ordered to attend because of some skill—such as myself and Lycomedes' stone-blind ancient rhapsode who sat with his lyre lying ready on the table beside him. Once again there was not the slightest sight or sound of any women either here nor—now I thought of it—anywhere in those sections of the palace I had visited so far.

I had no time to consider this, though it was hardly unexpected, as I was guided to my seat. This was at the far side of the room from the kings, but it allowed me to examine the impressive scale and dazzling decoration of the chamber I was seated in. Four painted wooden columns stood around the central fire pit, each one at a corner of the square opening in the ceiling above it. The ceiling itself was, if anything, more highly decorated than the floor, though the beautifully painted walls outdid them both—and far outdid King Peleus' great hall in Phthia. On and around the massive fire pit, a range of carcases were being roasted—a bull, two boars, sheep and goats. This was particularly impressive, for none of the animals being prepared at the fire pit was actually native to the island. Anything larger than a wild pony had to be imported from the mainland.

Having looked about the room, I glanced around the tables and established that my own seat appeared to be the lowest position available. It was certainly furthest from King Lycomedes, tucked away in a draughty corner by the door. But even with the damage to my eyes I had no trouble in examining the king. He appeared to be quite tall, though his elevated throne was designed to add to his consequence, as was the dazzling wall hanging suspended behind it. His actual frame was almost impossible to judge for it was hidden in formal robes that widened his shoulders and broadened his chest while hiding the girth—or lack of it—of his belly. The wrists and hands protruding from the gorgeous sleeves, however, were plump, which led me to speculate that the king was full-figured as well. This impression was confirmed by his face which looked like the face of a plump child, rubicund and cheery. He wore no crown and his well-trimmed hair was whiter and thinner than Nestor's. He had no beard, clearly preferring to leave his ruddy cheeks, jowls and chins clean-shaven. However, although his face and body suggested a cheerfully self-indulgent, wine-bibbing character, it was clear that the force of his intelligence was nevertheless powerful. Beneath the sweep of white eyebrows, two light brown eyes surveyed the room like those of a roosting eagle. This impression was compounded by the broad, beak-like hook of his nose—so different to the straight Achaean noses with which he was surrounded. However, I could see quite clearly perched on that elevated throne the kindly old king who had unhesitatingly welcomed Theseus to Skyros when the great hero and exiled king of Athens came here to retire from public life and farm some fields he happened to own on the island.

On Lycomedes' right sat Nestor and on his left sat Odysseus. Next to Odysseus sat Hypatios and next to Nestor sat the largest, most powerful man I had ever seen in my life. I knew who he was, of course. This was Ajax, son of Peleus' brother King Telemon of Salamis and Achilles' cousin. True, I had never seen the long-dead Hercules but I could hardly imagine he would have been any more massive and prepossessing than Ajax. I could certainly understand how one glance at that enormous seat in Peleus' grandstand overlooking his military display told Odysseus that Ajax had been there before him. The young giant towered not only over Nestor but even over Lycomedes on his elevated throne. His shoulders were far wider than Lycomedes' even without the formal robes, and the barrel of his chest would have held sufficient water for a voyage to Troy and back. His arms were larger than Elpenor's legs and I could only imagine what the legs beneath the table must resemble: ships' masts or tree-trunks, I supposed. On top of those herculean shoulders sat a short neck as thick as the columns beside the fire pit and on top of that a great, square head. A low brow was squashed between a thick brown hairline and heavy brown brows. Piercing brown eyes sat astride a short, straight nose ending in broad bull-like nostrils. Then a great cascade of hair, moustache becoming beard apparently without a break for a mouth. The beard, however, jutted forward, betraying the presence of a strong chin beneath it. The continuous cascade of moustache and beard became of interest almost at once, for, alone at the top table, Ajax was neither eating nor drinking. And as I realised that fact, so I saw that what flesh was visible between eyebrows and hairline, along cheekbones almost as circumscribed as his forehead, was pallid and disturbingly sickly-looking.

The feast proceeded in a highly formal manner. After an introductory pile of fat olives, tiny cucumbers and cheeses accompanied by various wines had been consumed, the palace cooks went seriously to work. The tenderest, most succulent joints of the king's preferred roast animals were placed in front of him and he indicated which particular morsels he wanted with all the obvious enjoyment of a child choosing honey cakes. These were carved for him and added to his serving. When King Lycomedes was satisfied, the massive portions he had selected were moved right and left as first kings, then princes, then lords indicated their preference and were served. So it went, on and on. There was a kind of inevitability to the fact that I ended up with a stringy pink piece of goat. I didn't need to demonstrate my preference—it was all that was left. I suspected I was lucky to get that and had only done so because Ajax refused everything which was offered to him.

iii

After the eating, there was formal drinking and cups were raised to Lycomedes as our cheerfully welcoming host, to the kings who were present, to the kings absent but represented by men such as Lord Hypatios, to the absent kings' representatives themselves, starting with Prince Ajax then Hypatios and so forth. I noted that Lycomedes' rhapsode was raising and draining his cup with the best of them so I was careful only to wet my lips as each salutation was called. After this ceremonial, the gifts were brought in. King Nestor's men came first as he was the senior guest. They brought in an enormous inlaid box which turned out to be full of extremely expensive gold- and silver-mounted jewellery: finger-rings, toe-rings and necklaces made of pearls imported from beyond the Hittite Empire, pendants and breast-pieces in all sorts of designs, hair-bands and head-bands both plain and adorned with strings of precious stones and jewels; bracelets, armlets and ankle bands studded with rare blue and green jasper from Egypt, and bloodstones, which some call heliotrope. And, most cunningly of all, perhaps, silver mirrors even more polished than the guard captain's armour. The king was apparently more than satisfied and put these aside when he had sorted through them, with many lengthy expressions of gratitude supported by yet more toasts. Nestor's servants were replaced by Elpenor, Perimedes and Euylocus. Odysseus' gifts could not have been more different. The massive oarsmen presented the king with a range of swords in ornate scabbards, fine bronze blades secured to grips of metal, bone, horn and wood by silver pins. Matching daggers were presented beside them. Bronze shields inlaid with jewels to match the ornate scabbards appeared, engraved with scenes from legend guaranteed to terrify any opponent. Helmets of all sorts, designs and materials from gilded bronze to boars' tusks sewn on leather. Tall spears made of ash wood, with vicious-looking points fashioned from rare dark iron and end-pieces made of bronze. Reticulated bows from the warlike East with arrows whose heads were smaller versions of the lay-out of his city. And, finally, a cuirass with matching greaves, all in bronze faced with gold and a high-crested golden helm to match. Again, the kindly old king was overwhelmed with gratitude, though he observed with great regret that he was far too old and fat to make use of any of the gorgeous weaponry these days—

even if he had to face the fearsome pirates of Lesbos. After all this, the final presents of brightly coloured wool and linen cloths, some of which also came from Egypt and the East, seemed all the poorer by comparison and Lord Hypatios seemed almost embarrassed to be bringing such meagre gifts from King Peleus, despite Lycomedes' courteous reception of everything put before him. But then it occurred to me that Peleus' original gifts—no doubt far more impressive than these—were still on the vessel commissioned with bringing Dion, his apprentice and Phthia's formal embassy to Lycomedes' court. Wherever that ship, and all those still alive aboard it, had vanished to.

These thoughts were interrupted by King Lycomedes himself, who had finished his examination of King Peleus' cloth. 'Rhapsode!' he called in a surprisingly strong voice. 'It is time for a song!'

The Skyronian rhapsode got rather unsteadily to his feet, felt around on the table until he found his lyre, then allowed himself to be led towards the fire-pit. As he searched blindly for his lyre I got a closer look at his face and was shocked to see a deep burn scar across the bridge of his nose and two more on the outer edges of his eye sockets. His eyelids were strangely thick and he had no lashes. It struck me with unsettling force that the man had been blinded on purpose long ago by someone pressing the blade of a red-hot dagger across his face. A stool had been placed by the fire-pit, at the base of the pillar closest to the king and his royal guests. The rhapsode sat on this, leaned back against the column, adjusted the formal himation he was wearing, placed his lyre on his thigh, struck a resonant chord and began his song:

Sing, muse, of the sweet whisper of the pine tree that makes her music by springs where naiads sport. And no less sweet is the melody of the pipe of Pan which awakes the lonely shepherd Endymion who calls to lovely Echo, nymph of the mountains...'

I felt relief wash over me. Not only was the king's rhapsode able to perform after all but it seemed he preferred pastoral songs. With a little luck, my epics would make a welcome change. I stopped listening as the rhapsode warbled on about nymphs and shepherds frolicking on the slopes of Mount

Olympus, seduced by the piping of Pan, much to the amusement of the watching gods, and began to go through my own repertoire of more heroic refrains.

My thoughts were interrupted, however—as was the rhapsode's song—by the abrupt departure of Ajax. The gigantic prince suddenly lurched to his feet and pushed past the guests seated next to him, nearly overturning the table in the process. He staggered drunkenly past the rhapsode, nearly knocking him into the fire pit and all-but ran out through the arch that I was sitting beside. He plunged blindly down the corridor beyond it, but slowed as he reached the far end, apparently uncertain of his way. Then he fell to his knees and pitched forward onto his face with a crash that seemed to make the whole place shake.

***

I was nearest, most sober and consequently the quickest thinking. Therefore I got to him first despite my limping legs. That was it, though. I could no more have turned him over than lift one of the gigantic blocks the citadel walls were made of. I was relieved but hardly surprised to discover that Odysseus was first after me. He had brought Elpenor and Euylocus with him and together they managed to turn Ajax onto his back. 'This looks bad,' said the captain. 'It's a long time since Chiron tutored me in the art of healing as well as that of fighting…'

'Even longer in my case,' added Nestor as he arrived at Odysseus' shoulder.

'So, it looks as though we need a court physician, and quickly—unless someone else has been with Chiron on Mount Pelion more recently than we have.'

The captain who had led me from the gate to my chamber appeared next. 'The court physician is the Egyptian Hesira,' he said. 'I shall have him summoned at once.' He called to a servant who was standing gaping in the corridor and despatched him with a few terse words.

'I believe eight men could lift the prince,' said Odysseus. 'Three each side with one for his head and one for his ankles. And if you will direct us, I think we could carry him to his chamber. It would be more fitting for this Hesira to tend him there in private rather than here beneath the eyes of the whole court.' I looked around at his words and I could see what he meant—even the cooks and servers had come through to see what was going on, and the king himself was no doubt on his way as well.

Ajax was raised shoulder high by Odysseus, his oarsmen and several strapping servants led by the guard captain. In the absence of anyone better qualified, I took his lolling head in my one good arm while Nestor took his ankles. The captain was about to lead us to his chamber when the rotund figure of King Lycomedes appeared in the doorway of the otherwise empty megaron and his voice echoed down the corridor. 'Lochagos Adonis, what is going on?' he demanded, giving the captain his full formal title.

Captain Adonis paused to answer his king. 'Prince Ajax has been overcome by some malady, Majesty.'

'Have you sent for Hesira? The poor young man must be tended at once.' The king came forward as he spoke.

'We have, Majesty.'

'Then carry the prince to his chamber. Hesira will meet you there.' Lycomedes turned down a side passage and vanished.

With Captain Adonis as our guide, we carried Ajax along the labyrinth of corridors to the room he had been assigned by his genial host. As we went, so Odysseus talked. 'I've never seen Ajax unwell. Not only is he spectacularly fit and unbelievably healthy, I've always assumed that anything which might cause him to sicken would in all likelihood be seen off by his massive frame.'

'Therefore,' I suggested, 'whatever has done this must be extremely powerful.'

'Hmmm,' he answered pensively.

'Oh I don't know,' said Nestor, 'when I was on the way to Colchis with Jason I remember even Hercules falling ill. In fact...'

This reminiscence was sufficient to take us to Ajax' chamber where we found a pair of his personal servants waiting. As with Elpenor and the rest of Odysseus' men, these were broad-shouldered, battle hardened crewmen, fitting to attend a great warrior such as their leader. They were surprised by the prince's state but by no means rendered helpless with shock. In stead, like Elpenor and the men bearing the massive body, they came forward looking for a way to help. Together with the men who had been carrying him, they laid Prince Ajax on his bed. As I had been in charge of the massive head, I stayed close by it even when it was lying safely on a rolled-up cloak. Nestor stood looking down at him with a worried frown, silent for once.

'The prince ate nothing at the feast,' said Odysseus, 'and only made a show of drinking the toasts as far as I could see. Did he have anything to eat or drink before he went through to the megaron?'

'Indeed he did,' answered one of the servants. 'An amphora of the finest wine was sent for the prince to enjoy as he readied himself.' The servant pointed to an ornate wine jar which was sitting on a table with an alabaster goblet beside it.

'Where did it come from?' asked Odysseus.

'We supposed it came from King Lycomedes. I'm pretty certain it was brought by one of his servants.'

'But no-one actually told you where it had come from?' said Nestor, and was answered by a shame-faced shake of the head.

'And the prince seemed fit and well before he drank it?' asked Odysseus.

'He was. And he seemed well when he left for the feast,' said the servant, glancing at his mate who nodded confirmation.

Odysseus picked up the goblet and sniffed it. He frowned. 'Then we had better find a way to make the prince empty his belly,' he said. 'Because it seems certain that whatever was in this originally is in his stomach now. And that is what is doing the damage.'

iv

Nestor stirred. 'The physician Hesira should be able to advise,' he said. 'Though I've never really trusted Egyptians myself. I remember King Idomeneus telling me about some Egyptian traders who came to Crete… Rogues and thieves the lot of them…'

Lycomedes' physician arrived at that point and if he heard Nestor's remarks he gave no sign. He was a tall, dark-skinned man with an extremely long neck, an angular face, a shaven head and the darkest eyes I had ever seen. Though clearly not of Achaean origin, he wore a Greek himation. He asked exactly the same questions as Odysseus had asked and came to the same conclusion. 'I have a tincture that will induce vomiting,' he said, his accent thick but his words perfectly understandable. 'Keep close watch on the prince while I go and fetch it.'

There was no problem about following Hesira's advice, for no sooner had he departed than the anxious king himself appeared once more with what seemed like most of his courtiers close behind. Ajax had been here for several days and it was clear that no-one else of consequence had visited until Nestor and Odysseus arrived, for the prince's chamber was larger and more beautifully decorated even than Odysseus' had been in Phthia. There was room for a good number of people to come and watch the prince's treatment. Odysseus caught my eye and we shared a flicker of a smile—we might just as well have called the physician to the passage where Ajax fell; there were even more onlookers in here now than there had been there.

A certain number of the visitors soon regretted their inquisitiveness, however—mostly those closest to the massive prince's sick bed. Hesira came hurrying back with a phial of liquid in his hand and an assistant carrying a large bowl close behind him. The physician and his associate pushed through the crowd of onlookers until they were beside me at the head of the bed. 'Hold his head,' the physician ordered and I obeyed as best I could with two strong hands but only one fully functioning arm. The boy with the bowl came closer still. 'Lift his head. Can someone support his shoulders?' said Hesira, seeing the difficulty I was having. Odysseus and Nestor obliged, reaching in from behind the bed-head to so. When his patient was half sitting up with his head steadily over the bowl, Hesira expertly took hold of the prince's nose. As soon as Ajax opened his mouth to breathe, the Egyptian poured some of the phial's contents through the moustache straight into it, released the nose and pushed the lower jaw up so that the mouth closed again. Ajax stirred, automatically swallowing rather than choking. Hesira turned to his audience. 'Now he said, I suggest you all stand…'

That was as far as he got. The huge prince's massive frame heaved. Hesira skipped nimbly back, the boy with the bowl leaned further forward. Such was the force with which Ajax emptied his stomach, however, and the enormous quantity of liquid which came out of him, that the bowl could not have held it even had the convulsions not jerked his head and shoulders out of our grasps. Everyone nearby was splattered, King Lycomedes only saving his gorgeous robes with an unexpectedly athletic backward leap. The room emptied long before the prince's final heave, leaving only Odysseus and Nestor still trying to keep those massive shoulders steady, myself—though I had lost control of his head long ago—Hesira, his helper and Ajax' two servants. The stench was dreadful; something about it made me think of mice. I could see the Egyptian's narrow nostrils twitching too and suspicion move toward certainty in those dark eyes of his.

'Hemlock?' wondered Odysseus when the prince at last settled back and conversation was possible once more.

'I fear so,' nodded Hesira.

'So it was definitely no accident. It was a deliberate attempt to poison the prince. We need to discover who sent him the wine because it certainly cannot have been the king!' Odysseus lowered his voice. 'And try to discover why anyone would want to poison the prince.'

Hesira nodded once again, his full lips thinning and his expression settled into a worried frown. 'We cannot easily move the prince so it is fortunate his bed remains unsoiled. I will clean his face myself and oversee the cleaning of the room. Even his vomit may be dangerous. Then I will collect some more potions in case he relapses and ask his men here to keep careful watch on him tonight. One failed attempt may lead to another, more successful, one.'

'That would be wise,' said Odysseus as he and Nestor, who also escaped befoulment because of their position behind the sick man's shoulders—as I had escaped myself because of my place behind his head—led the way carefully out of the room.

'One of us had better tell the king what we've discovered,'

said Odysseus.

'I'll do that,' said Nestor. 'We're not what you'd call old friends but at least we go back a long way. And of course as a member of Jason's crew I once knew Medea pretty well, and there was nothing she didn't know about poisons and poisoning...'

***

'And I'd better warn Lord Hypatios,' said Odysseus as Nestor bustled away. 'If there's murder afoot, he'd better watch out for himself.' He set of purposefully and I followed in his footsteps without a second thought. The first thing we did was to enlist the help of a couple of palace servants who were carrying lamps with steady and reliable flames to the sleeping chambers of some minor courtiers. On Odysseus' orders, they escorted us through the dark corridors to Lord Hypatios' accommodation in stead. Odysseus relieved one of them of his lamp and, calling the Phthian lord's name, we entered. But his room was empty. There was no sign of the man nor his sinister servants. The captain shrugged and returned the lamp. 'Where else might he be?' he asked. By way of an answer, the palace servants guided us to the most likely alternative locations where we thought we might find him. As we searched, we found ourselves passing through increasingly dark and empty corridors, past chambers where lamps had been extinguished and the snores of heavy sleepers reverberated. After a lengthy and exhaustive search, Odysseus gave up with a shrug. 'He'll just have to look out for himself,' he decided. He kept the lamp he had borrowed to search Lord Hypatios' quarters and dismissed the servants. 'I'm still worried about Ajax, though. I think I'll check on him one more time before I turn in.' He turned to me. 'Want to come?' The alternative seemed to be to try and find my way back to my own room through the labyrinth of corridors in the dark. A labyrinth where the monster in place of a legendary Minotaur might well be a murderer intent on murdering me. I nodded more forcefully than was strictly necessary and set off after him once more. I might have found the maze of corridors confusing, but my captain apparently had no such trouble. He led us straight to the prince's accommodation.

Ajax seemed to be resting well, his face and accommodation both clean and fragrant. His men were keeping watch. 'Did the physician bring the extra potions?' asked Odysseus apparently without a second thought. The two men exchanged a glance. They shared a shrug and shook their heads. 'He has not yet returned,' said one of them.

Odysseus frowned. 'But he left long ago, before we started looking for Lord Hypatios!' he shook his head. 'Though I can see he tended to the prince's cleanliness in the mean time. Even so, I'd better see what he's up to. Do either of you know the way to his quarters?' The man who had just spoken said, 'I do.' He took one of the lamps that were illuminating the chamber and led us out.

The captain and I followed the prince's servant along the dark corridors quickly and silently. Odysseus was pensive, tired and not at all talkative. I kept glancing at him but his attention seemed primarily to be focussed on the flame of the lamp he was holding. Almost unconsciously, we bunched together, keeping close to the unsteady brightness of the two tall lamp-flames. My eyes were bad enough with the bolts of brightness dancing at the edges of my vision, growing brighter and more frequent the more tired I became. Because of this, I was careful to look away from the flames themselves, preferring to watch the way our shadows loomed over us, reaching up the walls and across the ceilings. So, almost accidentally, my eyes became used to the darkness. I suppose it was because of this that I was able to see the brightness coming out of an open doorway quite clearly some time before we reached the room. I did not have to exercise any of my captain's logic at all to guess that the one bright doorway in the long dark corridor must belong to the physician, still hard at work, no doubt, preparing restorative potions for Prince Ajax.

'Is it much further?' demanded Odysseus abruptly.

The servant and I both answered at once, 'We're nearly there.'

But even as we answered, I thought I saw a flicker of shadow passing through the brightness, as though some dark spirit had flitted out of the place to vanish into the shadows. 'Captain,' I whispered. 'Did you see that?'

'See what?' he asked, glancing up from his pensive study of the lamp flame.

'I don't know,' I answered. 'A shadow, I think.'

'A shadow? What sort of a shadow?'

'I don't know... Of a person, perhaps. Someone in a long, dark robe. I couldn't see clearly and it was gone in a heartbeat.'

This conversation, brief though it was, took us to Hesira's doorway and the three of us entered together. The physician was seated facing away from us in a high-backed chair that rose to the level of his shoulders. He was sitting, immobile, apparently looking straight ahead at the piles of phials and tinctures on the table in front of him. His hands lay either side of the medicines, half-open and utterly still.

He would have been slumped forward, face down in the midst of them, I suppose, except for the fact that the dagger whose cross-guard was caught on the back of the chair was holding him erect as its blade ran into the nape of his neck, through his spine and the various tubes of his throat to protrude for a finger's length out at the front, supporting the weight of his lower jaw and holding his dead head high.

V

'That's one of the daggers I gave to the king,' said Odysseus. 'I had them all specially sharpened. How in the name of all the gods did it get here?'

He looked at the servant as though expecting an answer from him though I knew he was really talking to himself. Ajax' man was beyond answering in any case. He stood there, ashen-faced and shaking. I leaned forward and gently took the lamp off him for fear that he was about to drop it. 'He's... He's dead,' said the servant. 'I've never seen anything like it!'.

'If your flickering shadow was actually a person rather than your imagination or a trick of your eyesight,' said Odysseus to me, 'then it might well have been the murderer.' He reached out and felt the dead physician's cheek. I watched his hand with a kind of horror—which immediately intensified: I could have sworn the dead man's eyelid flickered.

'Captain!' I gasped. 'I think his eyes just moved.'

Odysseus moved round until he could see the physician's face full on. He gazed at the wide eyes for a moment. 'No,' he said at last. 'No movement there. But his skin's still warm. That makes it more likely that you did see the man that ran the dagger through his neck. You!' He turned back to the servant. 'You seem to know your way around the palace pretty well. We need to rouse the household! What's the best way to go about that?'

The servant stared mindlessly at the captain. His mouth moved as though he were drowning.

'Captain Adonis would probably be the best place to start,' I observed.

'Good idea, lad. You! Do you know where you can find Captain Adonis?'

'Captain Adonis?' repeated the servant, some semblance of understanding creeping into his words. 'I know where his quarters are.'

'Yes. Go and find him. Report what has happened and tell him I suggest that he rouses the household as soon as he possibly can. We must search out this murderer before he escapes or before he strikes again.'

The servant turned obediently towards the door but before he could leave I put the lamp back in his hand now that it was a good deal steadier. And he would need it to guide him through the dark and suddenly sinister corridors. The moment after he left, Odysseus was in action. He scoured the corpse and the chamber for anything that might add to our knowledge, such as it was, of who had done this. But there was nothing more for him to see and we had no time to indulge in further examination if we were to stand any chance of finding the culprit. He soon left the dead room at a fast walk, calling back to me as I limped after him as quickly as I could, 'Our main priority now must be to get back to Ajax as soon as possible because he only has one guard left. There is a murderer at work here; perhaps an associate of the man who murdered Dion and his apprentice. He's failed to kill Ajax once though it must have been him who sent the poisoned wine, and logic suggests most strongly that he'll try again while he has the time and opportunity. Remember, if you saw him escape into the shadows, he will have seen us approaching far more clearly. He'll know his time is limited therefore he will have to act quickly—or try once again tomorrow by which time the whole palace will be on the look-out and the proposition much more difficult and dangerous.'

Moved by the urgency of his own words, Odysseus started to run down the corridor, shading the lamp-flame with one hand in case his speed put it out. I did my best to follow him, but my leg simply would not allow me to keep up. Fortunately, when he finally left me behind, I was right at the beginning of the corridor that led up to Ajax' room. I saw him vanish through the distant doorway and, more certain of where I was and where the captain was, I slowed, trying to ease my cramped legs and catch my breath. The passageway in front of me was long and straight. I was cloaked in shadows at one end of it because the captain had the lamp. There was light spilling out of the open doorway at the other end. As with the passages below Peleus' palace in Phthia, there were openings along the sides that led either into other rooms or into yet more labyrinthine corridors. The slowing of my footsteps also had the effect of killing the sound my sandals made on the stone floor. As my breathing slowed, so even the hammering of my heart quietened. Although I was still dressed in my white linen tunic with pale face, arms and legs, I was cloaked in shadow now that Odysseus had taken the lamp away with him. All of which, I suppose, made me almost impossible to see and hear. A situation that became important when not one but two shapeless figures stepped silently out of the side corridor that opened closest to Ajax' room. Close enough to the brightness shining out through its doorway to be framed clearly and unmistakably against it.

***

I simply didn't know what to do at first. I gasped with shock. My heart lurched into that sickening rhythm once more. Frozen in place with my mind racing uselessly like a songbird flying round a cage, I stood and watched them. If they glanced my way they clearly did not see me. In stead they turned the other way and began to move slowly and silently towards Ajax' door. Horrific pictures and possibilities leapt into my whirling mind.

Whichever of them had killed Hesira had stolen one of the daggers Odysseus brought for King Lycomedes. They must have done so during the time that the megaron was left empty while everyone ran to see what the matter was with Ajax. What if they had stolen more than that lethal dagger? There had been matching swords—their blades far longer and probably just as sharp. None of the men in Ajax' room was armed or wearing armour. They would stand no chance at all against two swords, even ones wielded by women.

My reeling mind had taken me this far before I realised that one glaring fact. It had been there, right in front of me but I somehow missed it—like a hunter so focused on the boar in the bushes that he does not see the lion behind the tree. Whoever had murdered the physician and probably sent the poisoned wine therefore, and these two preparing to murder Prince Ajax and King Odysseus, were women! They were wearing the long eastern robes and veils demanded by King Lycomedes and favoured by his wives, concubines and daughters, their servants and slaves. I suddenly remembered King Nestor's comment, too: that he had known Medea—who killed and dismembered her brother dropping him piecemeal overboard to slow pursuit; who murdered her own children in revenge against the errant Jason then poisoned his new wife Glauce and her father Creon before making good her escape. Truly she was the witch-queen of poisoners! It was as though the monstrous woman was reborn, together with an equally murderous assistant!

'My Lord!' I called. 'Captain Odysseus! Look out!' As I spoke, I was in action, running as best I could up the corridor towards the murderous pair. They whirled, side by side, looking back at me. I knew the danger. If I was right about the swords I was a dead man. But I did not slow. 'King Odysseus!' I called again. 'Look out!'

The brightness from the door darkened and Odysseus was standing there. The women swung back to look at him. 'What…' he called.

They whirled once more, their robes spreading around them like black smoke and vanished back down the corridor they had come out of. 'After them!' rapped Odysseus. As though he was talking to me, I threw myself into the mouth of the passage, chasing the shadowy figures as best I could but I was soon overtaken by the price's servant. He carried a lamp which he kept slowing down to screen with his hand. Then Odysseus himself came past me, moving faster—less concerned about the flame of his lamp which flickered and died as he overtook the servant. But then I could see why this was. The passage we were following opened at the end into the outer air. Into moonlight and starlight, against which for a moment, two black shapes flickered like bats in flight. Odysseus' frame blocked the pallid moonlight next, then the servant's. Then, last, I came limping out into the night myself.

As I exited the shadowy constriction of that strange tunnel, my footsteps faltered. I slowed, then stopped altogether. I stood, stunned with awe at the vastness of the night. The servant must have known what was coming and Odysseus was too taken up with his hunt to pay attention to it. But it stopped me as effectively as a punch in the face. Or, rather, perhaps, a punch in the belly for I was simply winded. The passageway opened onto an area the same size as the courtyard, flagged in white marble like the walls. But this vast area was not walled. There was no balustrade or bulwark around its edges. It simply finished. And where it did so, the vastness of the night began. For this was at the very top of a mountain. The palace might be standing behind me, but in front of me there was only the marble flooring, the edge, then a vast nothingness stretching away and down—and upwards, indeed, to the stars and that huge, low moon. So entranced that I forgot about the strange figures, the servant, even King Odysseus. I walked forward, watching with simple wonder how the cliff which was still invisible beneath the white marble edge, allowed even my dim sight to travel northwards across a silver-surfaced bay hundreds of feet below, to the mountainous jut reaching towards Valaxa whose jagged crest swept away south-westwards seemingly just below the massive constellations of unnumbered stars.

I had no idea that I was walking like a blind man towards the edge until Odysseus' hand closed on my shoulder and stopped me in my tracks. 'They're gone,' he said. 'Vanished. Into the women's quarters. Take care I don't lose you too. That's a nasty drop.'

I looked down and caught my breath with shock. Just beyond my toes the marble ended and all that lay beyond it was a sheer dizzying drop straight down to the rocky shoreline of the bay so far below.

5 - The Women's Quarters

i

By the time we got back to Ajax's room, the whole palace was up and out. Captain Adonis left the sleeping prince under guard and led us through into the megaron where most of King Lycomedes' court and his important guests were assembled. They were keeping close to the fire pit for the still, clear night was chilly now. The vast majority of the crowd looked bleary-eyed and haphazardly dressed. This made Odysseus grunt with suspicion at the sight of the bright-eyed, perfectly turned-out Lord Hypatios when he appeared long after everybody else. 'Could he and his men have been flitting about the place disguised in women's clothes?' he wondered aloud, apparently speaking to me. 'Could they have brought hemlock with them from Phthia? They would hardly have had time or opportunity to find it here. And in any case I took the chance to look closely at the wine in the cup and the jar. I'm certain it was poisoned with a distillate rather than stems and leaves. The effects were far too powerful and rapid simply to be the result of soaking some plants in the wine. Besides, even Ajax would notice something amiss in wine whose bouquet involved actual flowers!' He sighed. 'And although my gifts are no doubt packed safely away in the armoury now, anyone could have stolen the dagger that killed the physician during the commotion around poor old Ajax when he first collapsed.'

'King Odysseus,' called an irritable Lycomedes appearing last except for Hypatios and most reluctantly, 'why have you roused the entire palace like this?'

Odysseus stopped his musings then and went over to explain matters to our host.

And so the next section of the night passed while the palace servants scoured the common areas for the mysterious murderers and the rest of us waited in the megaron. A contingent of cooks arrived and made up the fire in the fire-pit so they could produce food and drink for the noble assembly. A few people ate; many more drank. Time crept by. Hypatios finally arrived. The warmth from the fire pit made the already sleepy men assembled there even more somnolent. Soon, the vast majority were seated on the floor, beginning to doze. But while everyone was gathered drowsily round the warmth, I noticed Lycomedes slipping away apparently unobserved by anyone other than me. I looked around for Odysseus but he was deep in conversation with Hypatios. Neither man looked happy and it was obvious that I should only interrupt their discussion in the direst of emergencies. Nestor was sound asleep, no doubt dreaming of *Argo,* Jason and adventures long past with long dead heroes. My interest had been piqued, however, and so I followed the king, hoping that, as I seemed to be the only person who saw him go, I too would be able to sneak out of the room unobserved.

Lycomedes had vanished through an exit I hadn't even noticed before. This was not only because it was immediately behind his elevated throne with its high back but also because there was a wall-hanging there. The throne and the hanging conspired to cover the mouth of a passage. A narrow opening led into a cramped passageway, ill-lit by lamps standing in occasional niches along the wall. Lycomedes paused at the first of these and took the lamp from it. Then he hurried forward, apparently deep in thought. Certainly too preoccupied to notice me creeping from shadow to shadow, keeping my careful distance behind him, breathing silently and moving on tip-toe. I was being careful to stay quiet as our progress was taking us further away from the restless snoring of the crowd in the megaron and the bustle of diligently searching servants. I wondered whether I should also take a lamp and decided against it at once. However, even as the notion died stillborn, the king turned into a distant opening and vanished.

I tiptoed forward until I reached the opening the king had turned into. It proved to be the doorway into a large reception chamber. There were lamps in niches in the walls here too, and a circle of them on what looked like a chariot wheel hanging horizontally from the ceiling but even so the place was gloomy. I was just able to make out further openings in two of the distant walls which were also marked with sufficient flickering brightness to distinguish them from the dull stone surrounding them. There were various types of seating arranged around the walls but no-one was making any use of them. The king was standing in the middle of the space, face-to face with a figure dressed in long dark robes rendered anonymous by a heavy veil.

***

My heart lurched. The figure was identical to those I had seen earlier this evening, at least one of whom was guilty of murdering the physician. I tensed, trying to focus my weak vision on the figure's hands. Was there one of Odysseus' deadly daggers there? Was there a freshly-honed sword? When the arms stirred, I almost shouted a warning to the king but fortunately I managed to keep silent. The hands moved only to lift the veil concealing the figure's face and fold it back. The movement revealed the features of a woman. What struck me most about her was the strange combination of power and frustration. The light in the room was not good but I saw quite clearly that whoever this woman was, she was as used to command as King Odysseus, but for some reason she felt helpless at the moment. And this was seemingly nothing to do with the man standing opposite her.

'What is all this commotion about?' asked the woman. I might have had some trouble seeing her in any great detail but I had no trouble making out what she was saying. Her voice was low, but it carried: the voice of someone used to giving orders. The fact that she seemed to be addressing the king as an equal added to this effect. In her abruptness, indeed, she seemed to be treating him almost as an inferior. This was no slave or concubine, therefore; it must be a wife—and a senior one at that.

'There has been murder done and attempted murder,' explained the king.

'Dangerous enough to harm our plans?' she said.

'Possibly. As you know, the court is full of Agamemnon's emissaries at the moment. The timing could hardly be worse, independently of the fact that it was Prince Ajax who was poisoned and, it seems, King Odysseus who was instrumental in saving his life. Then he and his rhapsode searched the palace, discovered the second body, and caught a glimpse of someone dressed just as you are dressed now, as they left the murder room. Since then they have been chasing figures wearing women's robes around the palace as well.'

'Have you any idea who might be involved in such things?' asked the woman guardedly.

'Of course! And you know who is most likely to be roaming around the palace as well!' snapped the king. 'I wish I had never agreed to any of this. I never would have if I'd had the slightest idea how it would all turn out!'

The woman stood silently for a moment before she continued, 'And the successful murder?'

'Hesira the physician. Stabbed to death with one of the daggers Odysseus brought as a gift to me. Though it is clear that Odysseus himself could not have done the deed. He has apparently searched the physician's room and found nothing to reveal Hesira's murderer.'

'*Hesira*! That is madness! We were relying on him to tend Deidamia. To send medicines that would ease her sickness, at least, and let us administer them. Rhea can tend her as Rhea is apparently the only person the wilful little madam will allow anywhere near her. But Rhea is only the child's nurse not a physician; and elderly into the bargain. What shall we do?'

'I believe that the best thing to begin with will be to find a way to get our most unwelcome guests out of the palace for a while. Give us some space to breathe and to think how best to proceed.'

I was so caught up in this conversation that I did not hear the footsteps behind me. I didn't know anyone was there at all until a voice whispered, 'You do realise that it is death to be discovered here in the women's quarters?'

It was only by the grace of the gods that I managed to restrain a shout of surprise. I turned, and there was Odysseus. 'They think they know who it is!' I hissed. 'The murderer! They think they know!'

'It would be interesting to linger and hear more of what they know or suppose they know,' he breathed. 'In spite of the fact that they might well understand less about what's really going on here than they think they do. But I fear Captain Adonis will be arriving at any moment with news that the palace has been searched without result. In fact if we are caught here, the only people under serious suspicion will be you and me.' He turned and began to walk silently and rapidly back the way we had just come. As I followed, he threw a final comment over his shoulder which served to spur me on. 'And while I believe I would likely survive the outcome of such a discovery, I'm afraid you most certainly would not and I assure you that you do not want to face Lycomedes' favourite form of execution!'

ii

I caught up with Odysseus as he paused behind the curtain at the mouth of the passage, peeping round the edge and past the throne into the crowded megaron. Then with a swift, cat-like, movement he was gone. Holding my breath, I emulated him but my progress out into the room was more like that of a three-legged dog. It seemed neither of us was observed, however. This was at least made probable by the marked absence of Lord Hypatios who was in all likelihood the only other person wide awake there. But even as I followed Odysseus out from behind the table and paused at his side, to consider the implications of the absence of one vigilant man, another one arrived. Captain Adonis strode into the megaron with a squad of guards behind him. He came straight up to us without looking either right or left. 'We have searched everywhere except the women's quarters and found no-one,' he said to Odysseus. His tone was abrupt, bordering on the inappropriate.

The captain nodded and gave a weary smile. 'Well, as it was women we were chasing, and they vanished into the women's quarters into the bargain, that seems hardly surprising. The women's quarters were where you should have started.'

'We'll need the King's specific authorisation to do that,' Adonis said. 'And I'm not sure he'll be too pleased with the idea of a squad of soldiers poking around in his harem, his daughters' rooms or the private quarters of the female servants and slaves who tend them.'

'You can only ask,' said Odysseus. 'And choose your men

with care if he does give permission. Aphrodite forfend that there should be any inappropriate poking around in the women's private areas.'

Adonis remained as stony-faced as his guards. 'True,' he said at last. 'But at least in the mean-time we can rouse everyone here and send them back to their beds.' He did not add *And out from under my feet*, but he was clearly thinking it. He nodded to the squad who began to move through the room shaking the sleepers awake and explaining that they could get back to their rooms now. They had only just begun when the rest of the servants who had been searching under Adonis' command appeared carrying lamps with which to light the sleepy guests on their way.

Elpenor, Perimedes and Eurylocus wearily pulled themselves to their feet as the guards roused them and then they secured a servant with a lamp to lead the four of us back to our room. But before we could actually leave, a gesture from Odysseus stopped us. Lycomedes was sitting on his elevated throne, pretending to doze, just as though his sudden reappearance, like his disappearance, had never happened. Captain Adonis certainly seemed to notice nothing amiss as he approached the royal seat and roused the seemingly somnolent monarch. What they said to each-other was inaudible beneath the bustle of the stirring crowd around us, but they both looked pointedly across at Odysseus and we who were standing beside him.

Although I heard nothing of what was said, I did see the king's lips moving as though to pronounce a word I had heard earlier. 'Deidamia,' I said, giving voice to what I thought he had said. 'Who is Deidamia, Captain?'

'Deidamia,' said Odysseus glancing down at me with a frown. 'Princess Deidamia is Lycomedes' eldest daughter, the most beautiful of all his children and the darling of his heart.'

'Is she wilful?' I enquired, remembering the woman's description of the girl.

'Notoriously so. She apparently gets her strength of character from her mother Larisa, the king's senior wife and the lady you saw him talking to. Why?'

'She is unwell but will only allow herself to be attended by her old nurse.'

Odysseus nodded. 'Sick youngsters often seek the reassurance of a familiar face. Let's hope the illness is not serious.'

'Let's hope it's not the work of whoever has the distillation of hemlock,' I added. 'For whoever they are, they seem to have easier access to the women's quarters than we do. Or Captain Adonis does, come to that.'

So much of the night had passed that it seemed hardly worthwhile to go back to bed. The five of us stayed together, therefore; we four servants accompanying our king and captain to his private chamber where there was wine and water to drink but as yet nothing to eat. Unsurprisingly, we were all chary of drinking the wine, though it smelt perfectly fine. There was sufficient seating to accommodate us all, Odysseus and myself perching on the edge of his bed. 'Leaving Princess Deidamia on one side for the moment, the first thing it would be good to get clear,' said Odysseus, 'is whether the murders of Dion and his apprentice are part of whatever is going on here in the palace.' He was really just musing to himself, but we four all frowned with thought as we tried to reason an answer to his question.

***

'Surely,' I ventured, 'we should start by asking ourselves who benefits from the deaths. If someone somehow benefits from all the deaths and attempted murders so far, then it may not matter precisely where the murders took place. My own experience suggests this. The men who came so near to killing me in Troy were eventually caught because they started trying to sell the pieces of gold and silver they had stolen from me. They demonstrated that they benefited from the robbery and were found guilty of the act through possession of the items that had been taken. Furthermore, once they were held under suspicion it was soon proved that they had been active in other places and at other times.'

'What happened to them?' wondered Elpenor.

'Their leader was found guilty of all the other acts including murder. He was executed in the traditional manner: he was thrown off a cliff. The rest were imprisoned, fined and exiled.'

'But this case is not so clear-cut,' warned Odysseus. 'We have so far very little idea of what "benefit" the murderer might be expecting. Especially if the "benefit" in question is negative rather than positive. By which I mean that they may hope to stop something happening rather than to make it happen. At first glance, to stop Peleus and Lycomedes joining forces, presumably to stand against Agamemnon's attempts to drag them into the war he is planning against Troy.' He looked around the four of us, and clearly saw very little understanding on our faces. 'We can assume,' he explained, 'as I have mentioned already, that the killing of Dion and his apprentice was done by someone who wished to stop them bringing a lengthy and detailed message from Peleus to Lycomedes. But those murders only fit into the current situation if whoever did them was also trying to stop messages coming via Ajax and Hesira.'

'And,' added Elpenor, 'if the murderer has been able to get from the ships we last knew had beached on Skopelos Island, to the palace here. Difficult on the face of it as the vessels in question don't appear to have docked in the harbour at all.'

'Yes,' nodded the captain. 'As well as wishing for the outcome which we might call his "motive", our suspect—whoever that turns out to be—must have had the opportunity to commit the act. Which means,' Odysseus paused, picking up the thread of Elpenor's reasoning, 'that the ships *on* which or *near* which the first two murders were done have actually arrived at Skyros, though not in the same harbour as *Thalassa*, as you say. And the murderer has such freedom of movement that they have been able to get from whichever ship they arrived on not only into the city and the citadel but into the palace.'

'And into the forbidden women's quarters?' I wondered.

'Not necessarily so,' said Odysseus. 'I admit whoever is doing this, either as an individual or with a confederate, seems to go about wearing women's clothing and veils. But that by no means proves they are actually women. Or, therefore, that they are moving freely into and out of the women's quarters. Though of course that does remain a possibility. Moreover, it seems to me that any man—indeed any person—who has such freedom of movement between Lycomedes' harem and the common parts of the palace could only have such freedom if they had an unimaginably powerful hold over the king.'

'Would that explain the frustration expressed by Queen Larisa?' I wondered. 'She and Lycomedes seem to have been caught in the middle of some kind of a situation by these events which appear to be endangering their plans. Perhaps more than their plans. Could a couple of women hold such power, and create so much danger and confusion?'

Elpenor shook his head. 'Surely the culprit must be a man, whether he has such a hold over the king or not. I cannot conceive of a woman who would be willing or able to do such murderous things. Cutting a boy's throat, stabbing his master and pushing him overboard, attempting to poison Prince Achilles, stealing a dagger presented to the king and using it to murder his physician.' He shook his head. The others nodded their agreement.

Odysseus looked at them for a moment. 'Next time you bump into King Nestor,' he said, 'ask him to tell you all about Princess Medea of Colchis. He knew her well and is still trying to recover from the experience. No; I am certain that a woman might well be capable of these acts, were she driven to them by sufficiently powerful forces.'

'But,' I said, 'Surely the only woman we know to be closely involved in this situation, apart from Lycomedes' senior wife Larisa, Rhea the nurse and perhaps the sickly Princess Deidamia, is Queen Thetis. But we know the murderer cannot be her, no matter how she might be motivated, because she sailed north when Dion sailed south the day after Ajax left Phthia, a couple of days before we arrived. She went seeking Prince Achilles on Mount Pelion where he and Patroclus are extending their education. Besides, what sort of a hold could she have over King Lycomedes? It's inconceivable!'

iii

'Yes,' said Odysseus. 'I had forgotten that she sailed north. Still, it would be a good idea to try and find out what ships from Phthia did arrive here, when, where and who was aboard them.

From what we overheard King Lycomedes and Queen Larisa say, I don't think we'll have too much trouble in getting permission to leave the court for a while. Besides…' he fell silent, clearly deep in thought.

'Besides, Captain?' prompted Elpenor.

'Besides, when I was talking to Lord Hypatios I noticed something that struck me as strange.'

'What was that?' I asked.

'Horses. He smelt quite strongly of horses.'

'That's not so strange,' said Elpenor. 'There's a stable right beside the Harbourmaster's office. I noticed it when you sent me to talk to him about docking fees and so-forth.'

There was no real need for further discussion. The captain dismissed us to wash, dress and prepare for the day while he did the same, then sent a message to King Lycomedes. 'He's agreed,' said the captain as we all met up in the megaron later and he joined us in our basic morning meal of bread, oil, olives and cheese. 'We have the freedom of the island and as much of the day as we need. I must warn my rhapsode, however, that he will be required to practise his art at tonight's feast.' He looked at me with the ghost of a smile. 'So I hope you have a clean chiton as well as an outstanding song planned and you are ready to perform it, because you'll get no chance to rehearse today if you're planning on coming with us.'

Only the captain was used to horses. His men and I had had little experience of them but the owner of the stable had several mules and a donkey as well as a couple of work-horses and the powerful stallion he had hired to another aristocratic visitor the night before. He had also hired two of the mules to the lord's servants. The horse seemed pretty well-rested, as did the mules which had accompanied it. 'He can't have gone all that far or all that fast,' mused Odysseus, easing himself in the saddle. 'Perhaps a league; perhaps less. He can't have been out of the palace for that long either.'

'That's right, my lord,' the owner of the stable assured him. 'The horses, chariot and wagon are usually made available for them up in the palace. But the three strangers made use of the horse and the mules last night. A good price, and I was satisfied.

They promised they would stay on the flat and return the beasts by moonset, which they did, so they can't have gone all that far or ridden the animals too hard; not by moonlight even though the moon was full and very bright last night.'

These facts were of great relief to me—and, I suspected, to the others. None of us shared the captain's confident ease astride. In fact, in a covered area behind the stable itself there stood the wagon and the chariot side by side with tack for the work horses to pull them and I supposed that I was by no means alone in thinking of asking Odysseus to hire either one of these conveyances for us to ride in instead. But none of us did. We just mounted up and got ready to go. I was only grateful that my donkey's legs were so short that my feet were reassuringly close to the ground so I was not too likely to fall off. That was before I realised that it was not the foot-end of my legs that I should be worried about. I also felt the gods smile on me in the matter of my donkey's quiet and biddable nature. It seemed quite happy to follow the horse and the mules, thus requiring almost no guidance from my nervous and ill-tutored fists on its long leather reins. I was less certain about the gods' goodwill when my ride sprang into motion, however, bouncing me up and down in the saddle like a child enthusiastically bouncing an episkyros ball.

Almost immediately after we set out it became obvious that the direction Hypatios and his men must have taken was dictated by the terrain as well as by the moonlight and their assurances to the stable-owner. Unless the little troupe was riding mountain goats able to see at night, they could only follow the roadway leading down the centre of the valley that formed the wasp-waist of the island. On either hand, at varying distances, stood sheer mountain walls. The occasional precipitous valley reached mysteriously away between the peaks and one or two farmsteads sat perched high on the hillsides overlooking the broad, well-watered fields. The road we were following wound between these, allowing us a pleasant view of the kind of life Lycomedes' rhapsode, and indeed my own master Stasinus, loved to sing about. Except that there were hard-working farmers, their wives and families here tending their crops of almonds, lemons and olives; their pigs, goats and cattle. Weeding their fields of wheat and barley while their vines clothed the lower slopes. Their sheep grazed the higher ones, apparently with only the occasional shepherd in attendance and never a willing nymph, a randy faun or an amused deity anywhere in sight.

***

About half way across, when we had travelled perhaps ten stadia, we found ourselves riding through an untended and overgrown area. It was as well watered and fertile as all the rest, and should have been highly productive but apparently it had been let go to ruin. It was surprising to find this wilderness in the middle of so much abundant fruitfulness. The strangeness was further emphasised by the fact that there was a sizeable if derelict farm-house up on the vine-covered slopes overlooking the fields, seeming to watch them dejectedly as they ran so riotously to seed. 'It's so sad to see such neglected fields,' I said to Odysseus, just making a remark for something to say and not thinking all that much about it.

'These are the fields that belonged to Theseus,' he said.

'This is the farm he planned on retiring to after his exile from Athens all those years ago?' I asked, deeply shocked.

'The very same,' he answered. 'And I understand all was going well, even though a quiet island farm must have seemed like quite a come-down to one of the greatest and most popular heroes of all. Until the accident, that is.'

'The accident?'

'I thought you knew. You seem to know how most of his contemporaries met their ends. He was up there somewhere, apparently,' Odysseus pointed to the sheer slopes above the sorry-looking farm house. 'Surveying his new kingdom. Quite a step down as I said from his last one which comprised of Athens and the whole Attic peninsula. But by all accounts he was philosophical about his new position and looking forward to a quiet life as a farmer. Or at least that's what Lycomedes says. After all, he'd had adventures rivalled only by Hercules', and he'd managed to surpass even Hercules in some regards. He was certainly a great deal more popular. There was nothing more he wished to accomplish. He'd had enough of leading armies and ruling kingdoms. So he came here seeking peace and contentment. Then he really took a step down. Literally. As I understand it, he slipped when he was walking near the edge of a precipice. Unlucky rather than careless, unless he had managed to upset one of the gods, of course. But, over the edge he went. And fell. More than a stadion straight down onto a steep slope covered in sharp rocks. There wasn't much left of him when they found the body so I'm told. But Lycomedes had his remains sealed in a great bronze coffin fitting to house the body of such a man. Gave him a prodigious funeral. Terrible way for a great hero like that to go, though. Sent waves of shock through the whole of Achaea.'

This story took us to the end of the road where the valley we were following broadened and we all paused on a low ridge that backed the lazy slope down to the sea and looked around. On our left there was a craggy eminence with another citadel on top of it. There was a roadway accessing this up a steep gradient on the landward side, but on the seaward side its outer wall simply extended sheer black cliffs plunging straight into the surf. On our right, the distant hillslopes were less sheer and undulated away like great rocky green waves frozen in place. In front of us lay a double bay, two half circles divided by a short, fat isthmus. The bay on the right was empty but the left-hand one beneath the citadel, was providing safe anchorage for two ships. We didn't need the captain to point out that these were the two we were looking for; the ones Lord Hypatios had almost certainly visited by moonlight last night while we were searching the palace, half convinced that he might be the murderer dressed as a woman, while his two servants ran around the place, similarly disguised, planning to finish the job the poison had started on Ajax. There they sat, anchors down, oars shipped and sails furled, easily riding the incoming swell, a short wade out from the beach. 'It's odd,' said Elpenor,' but I could swear those ships are deserted.'

Odysseus gently kicked his horse into motion and we followed him down, dismounted stiffly and tethered our mounts by weighting their reins with heavy rocks, not that they showed much inclination to do anything other than crop the spiky, unappetising sea-grass there. Although the two ships made an arresting sight, the captain seemed more interested in the beach; to begin with at least. He strode down onto it with us all close behind him, then he stopped and looked around. The beach was narrow and rocky. Rocks no doubt extending out beyond the tide line explaining why the ships were anchored rather than run ashore. In between the rocks and pebbles, however, were the remains of two sizeable camps. Fire pits pocked the sand with their black throats in the midst of marks which could only have been left by tents. Two latrines dug, one on either side of the encampment. One part shielded by a makeshift wall of bushes. This beach was by no means as sandy as the others we had come across so far but it still gave a clear message of a hundred men or so who had come ashore and waited here. Almost certainly the same crews as had come ashore on Skopelos, with the same demands for privacy. But they waited no longer. Or, if they still waited it was neither here nor aboard.

iv

Odysseus looked up and down the beach. 'I can see plenty of footsteps showing where people came ashore from the ships and stayed on the sand,' he said. Then he turned. 'And although the place looks deserted, I can see the same footsteps treading a path up to the citadel. If they're not on the boats or the beach, that's where they must be.'

'Are you thinking of going up there to ask them what's going on, Captain?' asked Elpenor.

'Yes,' said Odysseus. 'It's the logical thing to do. But I'm going to inspect the ships first.' He turned to face the sea, where the ships' painted eyes stared unblinkingly at him. 'Ahoy the ships!' he bellowed. Then he put his hands round his mouth to form a trumpet. 'AHOY!' After a few moments when there was no reply, he turned to Elpenor and continued in his normal speaking voice, 'I'll take the boy with me. Do you all want to stay or come?'

Elpenor glanced at the others. 'We'll stay if it's all the same with you, Captain. We can guard your backs.'

'Guard our backs!' chuckled Odysseus as we waded out towards the first vessel. 'Lie on the sand, relax and gossip, more likely! It's a basic and timeless rule among the men in any crew or army I have ever served with: *Never volunteer.*'

The ships were larger than Odysseus' lean war vessel *Thalassa*. They were higher-sided and broader in the beam. Each one had a rope ladder hanging down the side so that the crew could get back aboard easily when they returned from wherever they were at the moment. Odysseus scrambled up the nearest then reached back down to lend me a hand. The first thing I noticed as I stepped aboard was that this vessel was fully decked. From my new vantage point I could see that her sister was as well. I was used to decked ships, freighters from my father's fleet. So, while the captain gave the main deck a cursory inspection, I found the hatch that led to the main companionway aft and raised its cover. Had this actually been one of my father's ships, there would have been a much larger hatch here and another larger still on the foredeck to allow cargo to come aboard and go ashore. This kind of access was facilitated by the fact that there were no oars or oarsmen on cargo vessels: Father's fleets were entirely reliant on the wind. But this was no more a freighter than it was a warship; it seemed like something in between. I went down the ladder into the below-deck area. It was quite bright in here because the oar-holes were all open and the oars retracted, lying across the benches from side to side. Further back on this level there were accommodation areas, and I suspected there would be similar but smaller areas at the narrow bows, for storage if not accommodation. Below the hatch in the main deck was another that opened down from the oar-deck. Below this in the dark and smelly area just above the bilge where the equipment needed for overnighting ashore was kept together with spare cordage, rope and squares of linen to fix the sail, I discovered something I was not expecting. I found it because of a couple of circumstances which proved that the gods were smiling on me. A beam of light fell vertically from the hatch in the main deck straight through the hatch in the oar-deck. It was bright enough to show me that the overnighting equipment was all gone, which was hardly a surprise given the state of the beach and the crew's continued absence. But what I found was also revealed because it had just been dropped from the oar-deck without much thought. It lay on top of the cordage and spare sail-sections, strikingly out of place. Two bags which had just been slung down here. They had not been hidden, just discarded together with a couple of tunics, sandals and a formal himation robe.

I carried it all up onto the main deck where I found the captain standing looking thoughtfully at his closed fist. Closer inspection showed me that a length of silver chain was hanging down on either side of his clenched fingers. I began to speak, but he unclenched them to reveal a tiny silver amphora. 'It's full of oil scented with sandalwood and myrrh,' he said 'Such as a woman of the court might anoint herself with. Lost sometime during a hurried disembarkation I suspect. Now what have you found?'

I showed him. Each of the bags I had found contained a lyre. One even simpler than mine and suited to an apprentice, the other a much more complex and beautiful instrument – the lyre of a master rhapsode.

***

'So, said Odysseus as he looked at them pensively. 'Now we know which ship Dion and his apprentice were on to begin with. Which ship they both died beside. And that at one time or another there may have been women aboard as well. But who else has been aboard and who was it who wielded the fatal knives?'

Our search revealed little else, much like the search of Hesira's room. The ships were no more designed to accommodate crew or passengers overnight than Odysseus' *Thalassa* was. If for any reason it was necessary to stay aboard at sea in the dark hours, the oarsmen would have to sleep at their benches and the sailhandlers on the oar-deck between them. The captain, navigator, any senior officers or any important passengers would bunk down in the basic cabin beneath the steering board aft. This was the only area aboard not given over to storage of one sort or another. If there were personal possessions aboard other than those no longer needed by the two dead men, then they had all been taken ashore with their owners. But it was obvious to both of us that the two cabins aft of the oar-decks would have provided ample housing for a good number of women if they wanted privacy while they were aboard.

But where were the women and the crews who had brought them here?

We waded ashore, laden with the bags and clothing. I loaded it over my donkey's withers then woke up Elpenor and the other two oarsmen who were apparently able to guard our backs in their sleep. As I did this, the captain took one last look at the beach and the hard mud roadway leading down the slope towards it. My own cursory glance revealed nothing more than the faintest scarring of footprints, slightly deeper hoofprints, their presence confirmed by the occasional pile of horse dung whose age suggested our own visit today, Hypatios' visit last night and other visits earlier still. I was pondering this when Odysseus called, 'That's enough. Mount up!'

We mounted up stiffly and trotted up the pathway to the citadel. We could see from some distance away that the gates were open. From closer at hand we could also see that they needed repair, sagged crazily and would not close anyway. Moreover, they were unguarded. But then, we were no invading army, hardly even a group of piratical sea-raiders. There was no need to guard the place against us nor indeed to give any warning of our approach. Which was just as well. Like sparrows in an eagle's nest the two crews managed to occupy hardly any of the space. They had erected their camp between the well and what must once have been the citadel's cooking area. They might not have been Myrmidons, but they were oarsmen and warriors of the Phthian forces. Although they were idle enough now, they had clearly been busy earlier. In process of being butchered for the fire, there were pigs, good-sized herons and what looked like a small wild horse as well as a variety of fish including a pair of fat dolphins.

A couple of the oarsmen looked up, with little interest to begin with, but as soon as they recognised Odysseus, a stir ran through the assembled men and they began to pull themselves to their feet. Odysseus swung himself off his horse and strode a little stiffly towards them, nevertheless achieving a slight swagger. He became a man amongst men; indeed, a captain among sailors. 'Are you well set here, men?' he boomed. 'You want for nothing? Lord Hypatios has seen to your comfort while you wait?'

These apparently simple questions cunningly established him at once as an intimate part of whatever was going on. 'I see he has arranged for the pigs and the dolphins to be delivered from the royal kitchens, quite a load even for the cart, though you've done well with your own hunting by the look of things; as long as that horse meat tastes as good as it looks! Will you need anything more in the near future? Any messages I can pass along?'

'No, Captain,' the self-appointed leader of the men looked over his shoulder. There was a general shaking of heads amongst his companions.

'You don't want me to replace the women, then?' asked Odysseus with a wink.

'No, Captain. They never had anything to do with us in any case. They were passengers, not playthings. We steered as clear of them as we could.'

'Of course, of course. Too good to mix with common oarsmen and sailhandlers, eh? Neither on one ship nor the other.' As Odysseus said this, I was struck by something I should have noticed earlier. Oarsmen and sailhandlers were all that seemed to be here. There were no women—as had been immediately obvious. But there was no-one clearly in command as Odysseus so obviously was aboard *Thalassa*. There didn't even seem to be a pilot or steersman, the second most important officers aboard. It looked as though it wasn't just the women, whoever they might be, who had been spirited away. But as I thought of this, I sensed something else as well. The atmosphere was changing; cooling. There was just the faintest frisson of suspicion in the air.

'That's true, captain,' the spokesman said guardedly. 'Though hardly surprising.'

'Quite. Quite. But the disappearance of the rhapsode and his apprentice must have surprised all of you who were aboard the same ship?'

'A mystery to be certain, Captain. Two mysteries indeed. But nothing for common oarsmen and sailhandlers like us to concern ourselves with. So we were told.' The man's tone was becoming suspicious now. Odysseus had clearly pushed his luck that little bit too far—had his fortune been *Thalassa*'s sail, he would just have lost the wind.

V

Odysseus felt the change of mood as clearly as I did. 'Ah, well,' he said. 'As long as Lord Hypatios has seen you comfortably settled. Let's hope he had made sure the women were as comfortable, eh?'

'It wasn't Lord Hypatios who brought the food and took the women,' said the sailor. 'It was Captain Adonis. And he led our captains and pilots away with them as well as a good number of crewmen. If you want to know any more, Captain, perhaps you had better talk to them.' There was an air of finality in his tone. When he stopped speaking there was something about his silence that reminded me of the walls of Priam's citadel at Troy: overwhelming and impregnable. He turned away and so did all the others. I suddenly realised that they were scared to tell us more. More than scared; terrified, perhaps, that they had told the wrong man too much already.

'So, Lycomedes is directly involved with the ships and their passengers,' said Odysseus as we rode back towards Skyros' main port and major city. 'And not just in terms of hosting Agamemnon's emissaries. Precisely how does it involve whatever the situation Queen Larisa was discussing with him? Who are the women Captain Adonis removed from the ships and where are they hiding now?'

'Surely they must be hiding in the women's quarters,' I said. 'It's the most obvious and convenient place. And, now I think of it, I was disturbed when we first arrived by the way we were all being watched as we walked up from the port to the palace. Do you think Lycomedes could be hiding the officers in selected houses in the city rather than trying to keep them out of sight at the court?'

'It's possible,' said Odysseus. 'Probable, even. But *why*?'

After a while, the way the two lyre-bags kept jarring against my knees prompted me to change the subject and bring up something that had been worrying me ever since I first noticed it. 'Did anyone notice Lycomedes' rhapsode's face?' I asked. 'The fact that he's been blinded on purpose?'

'Yes,' answered Elpenor. 'I did. I asked one of the servants about it. Nasty story. They all call the rhapsode Actaeon now though I don't know his original name. Actaeon after the huntsman who went into a forbidden grove in the forest and caught the goddess Artemis naked at her bath. In the story he was torn to pieces. Lycomedes' version is worse, if anything. Apparently the rhapsode found a way of going into the forbidden areas of the harem. He fell in love with one of Queen Larisa's handmaidens. Don't ask me how, given the way the king keeps the women hidden away and wrapped up in those veils and robes. But he did manage to get in there, meet a woman and fall in love. And she fell in love with him. They started seeing each-other in secret, somewhere in the women's quarters, so they say. Until one night they were caught. Lycomedes was outraged and decided to make an example of them. He had the whole court assemble on that big open space at the top of the cliff behind the palace. He ordered a brazier and he heated a dagger until it was almost melting. He had the lovers brought to the very edge of the ledge, then he personally pushed the woman over and ordered the dagger pressed to the rhapsode's face so that the last thing he would ever see was his beloved falling down that cliff to her death on the rocks below.'

Speechless with horror at Elpenor's brutal tale, we trotted on in silence until we reached the overgrown wilderness that had once belonged to Theseus. Then, as though his thoughts were simply too much to keep silently in his head, Odysseus started speaking. 'Of course the only women involved with Peleus' ships are Queen Thetis and her handmaidens. It seems most likely that they set sail for Mount Pelion or rather that they let everyone believe Pelion was their destination. Then they turned round and caught up with the ship carrying Dion and his secret message to Lycomedes.' He paused and rode on in silence for a few more moments, ordering his thoughts. 'If this is so,' he continued, 'we can only assume that Queen Thetis' desire to stop the message was even greater than her need to find Achilles. And she, or someone with the same motive, certainly did stop the message. While the two ships sat side by side on that beach in Skopelos, the apprentice died in case the rhapsode had shared the message with him. The footprints of whoever carried and buried his corpse were even smaller than yours, lad. Two women, therefore. Which also might explain the shallow grave. Then at least some of the women moved from one ship to the other and, soon after they sailed, while still in the grip of that westward current we had to fight to free *Thalassa* from, Dion was stabbed in turn and pitched overboard. By the gods' good graces he found the wreckage to cling to and so was swept round the north of Euboea Island and under our bows as we sailed from Aulis to Phthia even though he had bled to death long before we found him. And so the two ships came secretly to Skyros.

'Where, by some prompting I can not yet explain, King Lycomedes sent some of his most trusted guards to help them, to feed the crew while they waited on the beach then in the ruined citadel, and to give the officers, some of the crew and their female passengers shelter. Of course it is the female passengers who are at least part of this. Or rather, not the females themselves but the queen they serve. Thetis must be at the heart of this. Queen Thetis said she would sail north to Mount Pelion in search of Achilles. Instead she turned south, met up with the vessel carrying Peleus' messenger destined for Lycomedes.'

***

'What could the message have been, if stopping it was even more important to Queen Thetis than finding Achilles?' I wondered aloud. 'It must be that the two old kings have been conspiring to arrange for Achilles to lead his Myrmidons at Agamemnon's side after all. To send Achilles and his men instead of leading their own armies to Troy. Surely, Captain, you cannot have been the only king who realises that

Agamemnon's Trojan expedition is more likely to take years rather than months. That if it does, it will probably ruin the kingdoms of any kings who accompany him, whether they survive the encounter or not.'

'The boy has a point, Captain,' said Elpenor. 'Both Peleus and Lycomedes are old. The lines of their succession are uncertain. If they send sons to represent them, they might father more sons in the meantime if the ones at Troy die, though Lycomedes has only fathered daughters so far and we all know the trouble Peleus has had just getting one child. And if they send someone else, at least they will still be there to ensure that their kingdoms remain safe and secure.'

'Nestor can afford to come to war,' I added. 'Pylos is rich. Its slave women tend the reedbeds, strip, dry, spin and weave the flax that becomes the linen for our clothes and your sails. He can afford to take his sons, Princes Pisistratus, Stratichus and Thrasymedes with him to the war because he can still rely on young Prince Aretus to look after things during their absence. Peleus and Lycomedes do not have that freedom of movement or anything like it.'

'Besides,' mused Odysseus, 'there seems little doubt that Ajax, Pisistratus, Stratichus and Thrasymedes at least, are burning with desire to get onto the battlefield and earn reputations to rival those of the past heroes. And there is little doubt in my mind that Achilles is equally keen to go with them. More so, indeed. All his friends and relations of the same age and generation such as Nestor's sons and even his cousin Ajax would come to Agamemnon's war alongside armies supplied by their fathers. Only Prince Achilles would arrive at the head of his own army. The army that is likely to be the best army involved. He will answer Agamemnon's call, he and his Myrmidons, unless he can be stopped. And the one person with most invested in stopping him is his mother.'

But,' I said, 'all the others have mothers as well as fathers! Even if Achilles is her only son, what is it that drives Queen Thetis to such an extreme to save him from going to war alongside Agamemnon?'

'That's another story I'm surprised you haven't heard,' said

Odysseus. 'Achilles isn't Queen Thetis' only son. He's actually her seventh son.'

I gaped in surprise and confusion. 'Her seventh son?' I said at last. 'Achilles is her *seventh* son?'

'He is. But all the others died at birth. Imagine how that must have affected her. Six dead babies one after the other, then one that lived. Lived to become the most beautiful and talented youth of his generation. The pride of any parent's heart. The most precious gift the gods could ever give. And now he wants to go to war alongside his peers, friends and relations. He seeks to make a name that will echo down the ages like those of the earlier generations he wants to emulate—perhaps to surpass! Like Hercules, Theseus, Jason and the rest. To make himself immortal.' He paused, lowered his voice and then continued. 'While Queen Thetis is absolutely certain, that if he goes with Agamemnon, he will unquestionably be slaughtered beneath the walls at Troy!'

6 - The Seventh Son

i

'So,' I said, 'Queen Thetis is happy to leave Achilles and Patroclus safely on Mount Pelion with their tutor Chiron while she personally stops the two old kings putting their plan into action and sending Achilles off to war instead of them. And she is, as we speak, with her women hidden somewhere in Lycomedes' impenetrable harem, making certain that the old kings' stratagem comes to nothing, even if they have to kill in order to do so.' I fell silent for a moment, lost in thought. 'Which explains why Ajax was poisoned. Because Ajax like Dion could well have been carrying a message to Lycomedes, even though he set out for Skyros first. And I guess Hesira the physician met his end because he cured Ajax. But still, I can't imagine how she has forced Lycomedes to become a part of her plans. Especially as her intention is to forestall his aims at any cost.'

'I see three possible reasons,' said Odysseus. 'First, everyone has secrets and I assume Queen Thetis knows what Lycomedes' most dangerous secret is. Or, secondly, he is going along with her demands for the moment because he believes he has a way he can outwit her in the end. Or, thirdly, there is an element in this situation that we haven't understood or made allowance for.'

'If she's holding some threat over him, which seems to be most likely, then it must be potentially very damaging to his country and his kingship,' I said.

'Or to his personal standing and reputation,' nodded Odysseus. 'Which, as we can all see, are enormously important to him. He loves his royal rituals, his power, his unquestioned authority. The respect he enjoys throughout Achaea; the way in which even other kings are a little jealous of him and his harem full of the loveliest women, slave and free, anywhere in Achaea. So it must be something that will cost him all of this. Some revelation that he fears even more than falling-in behind

Agamemnon and leading an army across to Troy with Peleus at his side instead of Achilles.'

'Which we all agree would be potentially disastrous for any kingdom whose king does go to Troy. Even for your kingdom of Ithaca, Majesty, though it seems that your situation is far stronger than most, with the possible exception of Nestor's at Pylos. Although your son Telemon is far too young to take over from you, your wife Penelope is capable of holding things together for you. Famously so.'

'And in the unlikely event that Penelope needs any help or advice in my absence,' said Odysseus, 'her father Icarius and her mother Periboea both still live quite nearby in Sparta and would be happy to oblige.'

Odysseus fell into a brown study. His silence lasted until he turned off the roadway and led us into the stables where we returned the horse, mules and donkey. Before we left, Odysseus crossed to the outside shelter where he examined the cart and the chariot more closely. 'Captain Adonis,' he said to himself. 'I can see how he could fill this cart with carcases to feed the sailors as soon as notification of the ships' arrival at the far side of the island came through, and just about imagine how he might find room for five or so women seated in here for the return journey. But he took the chariot as well, and I can only see one reason for that. Queen Thetis would no more ride in a cart than allow herself to be spitted and roasted like its previous occupants. And Hypatios and his men visited the sailors from Thetis' ships last night. I'm beginning to wonder whether our Phthian lord is actually in league with his queen rather than with his king.'

'Is that important?' I wondered.

'Possibly. But let's stick to the matter in hand for the moment.' He turned to the stable owner. 'On the occasion that Captain Adonis took these, did you see any women riding in them?'

'No. He and his men took them empty and returned them empty.'

Odysseus straightened and looked up the hill towards Lycomedes' citadel. 'Took them up to the palace for loading and, in due course, for unloading.'

'Does that prove anything?' I asked.

'Only the depth of Lycomedes' involvement,' he said. 'Captain Adonis had to be acting under his king's orders. There's something about that which doesn't sit right. Something we're still overlooking.' He shook his head and strode out of the stable, with we four following hard on his heels.

***

As we passed the harbour, which was quiet now as most of the fishermen were out at work, a sailor from Ajax's ship *Nerites* approached us down the jetty. 'Majesty,' he called to Odysseus. 'What news of the prince? We heard he was taken unwell.'

Odysseus stopped. 'He was extremely unwell, but to the best of my knowledge he is much better now and likely to be improving rapidly.'

'And all is well in the palace? We have witnessed some strange comings and goings. One of our watch-keepers is even certain that there are men from the ships anchored on the far side of the island hiding somewhere in the town. But we haven't seen them and he might have been drunk when he thought he saw them creeping through the dark. Your harbour watch on *Thalassa* saw nothing. It's as though some sort of spell has been put upon the place.'

'A spell? Who would put a spell on anyone here?'

'The dark queen. Thetis. We spied her three nights ago, all in black, riding up to the palace in her chariot. Too much like Medea for my taste.'

'And was this chariot pulled by dragons like Medea's?'

'No, Majesty. It was pulled by horses and driven by the captain of the palace guard. But even so…' He shrugged. 'We've not been surprised to hear of strange things going on up there ever since!'

Odysseus turned to me as the sailor hurried back towards his ship. 'And there, my boy, you see how legends start. Then they end up in your heroic songs, complete with magic spells, fabulous beasts and Olympian gods. Queen Thetis' chariot will be pulled by dragons in stories soon enough, I'll wager. Just like

Medea's. The pair of them seem to be getting too much alike for my peace of mind.'

'You mean you think that Queen Thetis personally cut the boy's throat, stabbed Dion, poisoned Ajax then murdered Hesira?'

'It's beginning to look like it, isn't it? Who else could get two women to carry a body up off a beach and bury it beneath a bush in the dunes?' said Odysseus grimly. 'She sounds like someone who will stop at nothing and who doesn't mind getting her hands dirty.'

We climbed the hill slowly after that. The captain said it gave him time to think but I knew he was making sure I didn't get left behind, especially as my limp had been compounded by stiff hips and a sore backside courtesy of my donkey-ride. It also gave him the opportunity to look around in the daytime go-to-market bustle to see if he could spy anything unusual or amiss. But, like the harbour watch on his ship, we saw nothing. It seemed that the drunk sailor from *Nerites* had been imagining things. Meanwhile, Elpenor carried the bags with the lyres; Perimedes and Eurylocus split the tunics, sandals and himation between them. The clothes were clean and neatly folded. I was planning on wearing the himation for my performance tonight. I didn't think Dion would mind.

Odysseus' brief conversation with the sailor from Ajax's ship put the sickly prince in the forefront of his mind. This was obvious because as soon as we arrived in the citadel, he walked determinedly towards Ajax's room. Elpenor and the others went to put Dion's lyre and clothing in our room and waited there for further orders but I followed the captain, fascinated to see what he would discover or deduce next. Ajax was up, if not yet fully recovered, and pacing his room, much to the disquiet of his guards who had been ordered by Adonis to keep him safe and who obviously interpreted that as meaning they should keep him imprisoned there for his own good. They recognised Odysseus, however, and were happy to let him overrule their captain. Having been dismissed, they went off in search of Adonis while Odysseus and the milk-pale Ajax walked slowly out onto the big marble-flagged ledge behind the palace. They paced up and down there, deep in conversation, apparently paying no attention to the seemingly limitless vista encompassing them or the vertiginous drops that surrounded them on three sides. They were far too interested in what they were saying to each other to note the wind which tugged them relentlessly toward the abyss. I limped a little way behind them, concentrating on their conversation too, rather than on the dizzying cliffs that so strangely tempted me towards the edge. And forcing to the back of my mind any thoughts of the blind rhapsode Actaeon's final vision of his lover hurtling down towards the distant rocks below.

'Peleus gave me no particular message for Lycomedes,' rumbled Ajax. 'He knows my memory for such things is not very reliable.'

'I would half expect him to risk something simple, though,' countered Odysseus. 'Then send the more complex afterthoughts with Dion hard on your heels. After all, you are one of his strongest supporters, just by your very existence. You're really keen to go to Troy and if you can find your cousin Achilles and persuade him to go with you that's all to the good as far as Peleus is concerned.'

'It puts me in the opposite camp to Queen Thetis, though, and that's obviously a dangerous place to be,' said the massive prince, though he did not sound particularly fearful to have found himself in that position, even though it nearly cost him his life. 'When I am over the effects of whatever was in that wine, I might have a bone to pick with her. I know she was less than happy that I saw through that charade she made Peleus stage for my benefit where the Phthian army took on the Myrmidons and apparently fought them to a standstill.'

'Yes. Peleus showed us the same thing, even though she was gone by that time.' Odysseus nodded.

'The idea of the entire set of manoeuvres is that we'll take the message back to Agamemnon that a Phthian army could perfectly well replace the Myrmidons so he doesn't need to keep looking for Achilles after all. But she can be pretty certain I'll do no such thing. Though I must admit I wasn't expecting to get poisoned wine as my reward.'

'But perhaps that's what gave her a motive to kill you, lad: for seeing through the military charade rather than suspecting you of carrying secret messages.'

'I suppose so.' Ajax shrugged philosophically. 'Unless, as a third option, she thinks I know where Achilles actually is and stand a chance of recruiting him after all. I suppose I can understand how she'd kill to stop that, as we seem to be coming round to increasing certainty of her guilt in the matter.'

I must admit I shook my head in silent wonder that Ajax should view such a murderous attempt on his own life so calmly and reasonably. It was something to do with the soldier's lot, I supposed. Thanatos and Ajax were old friends and he planned to become even better acquainted with the fearsome god of death under the walls of Troy. In the mean time he could shrug such near misses off. Even so, I would not have liked to be in Queen Thetis' sandals if these two could ever prove conclusively that her hands had poured the poison, wielded the knives and slit the throat.

'But everyone knows where Achilles is,' said Odysseus, in that strange, testing tone that made what seemed like a statement into a question. 'He's where his mother originally went to seek him. He's on Mount Pelion.'

'No. I don't think he is. I took the opportunity to go up to see Chiron before I arrived at Phthia. The old man was chary and tight-lipped but I didn't get the impression that Achilles was on Mount Pelion at all.'

'So, if Achilles isn't on Pelion, then where is he?'

ii

Dion's himation robe was too large for me but I managed to carry it off pretty effectively, I thought. I arranged it carefully as I sat on the rhapsode's stool, feeling the heat of the fire-pit warming my right shoulder, and looked around the megaron at King Lycomedes and his guests. All the chairs were full except Ajax's who had sent his apologies; though he was up, and strong enough to walk and talk, his stomach was still too unsettled to face food or drink. He was, perhaps, the wisest of us all. The evening meal had been served early and underdone. Had my goat been any less cooked it would have run bleating for the door. There had been far fewer toasts and libations than yesterday even though there was much to celebrate, not least that the absent Ajax had returned almost magically from the bank of the River Styx. Furthermore, I had been informed that I was required to recite my shortest epic, for I was only a part of the evening's entertainment and not a very important one at that.

I finished arranging my new himation, therefore, closed my eyes, uttered a swift prayer, and struck the strings of my lyre. The only thing likely to lengthen my performance was one of King Nestor's stories. And my finest poem, the one best suited to the setting and the occasion, was the one that tempted him most sorely to start telling them:

'*Sing, Muses, of the anger of Hercules, black and murderous, costing the Trojans terrible sorrow, casting King Laomedon into Hades' dark realm leaving his royal corpse for the dogs and the ravens. Begin with the bargain between the old king and Godlike Hercules. Strong promises the old king broke calling forth the rage of the son of Zeus…*'

My recitation seemed to be well received but it was clearly of secondary importance. The main event was to be the famous dance performed by the young maidens of the royal harem. Not the wives or concubines, but the beautiful daughters; their loveliness wasted as far as I was concerned because they performed their renowned and intricate dances wearing the heavy veils they always wore when moving in masculine society.

As the applause for my song died and I returned to the low seat in the draughty corner by the opening into the corridor, a group of royal musicians arrived. My rhapsode's seat by the fire pit was usurped by a young man with a kithara which was far more complex than my own simple lyre and a lot more like the one Dion had played. It was clearly pre-tuned and he ran the fingers of each hand over the strings as the others clustered round him. There were two men each with the double-flute aulos which came together at the lips but spread apart so that each pipe could be individually played by each hand – two men effectively playing four instruments, therefore. The flute-plyers were joined by another pair, each with a tympanum on whose taut leather drum-head they could beat out a regular rhythm with a short drum stick. But most important, I calculated, were the four youths each holding a set of koudonia copper bells. These supported the drums keeping the flutes and harp in rhythm, but the tinkling sound they made was simply magical. As soon as the musicians were assembled the rhythm established and the kithara joining the aulos in producing a melody, the dancers snaked in—coming so close to me as they swept by that I felt the breeze of their passing on my face and my nostrils were filled with the scent of their perfume.

Dazzled by the brightness of their amazingly colourful costumes, I watched their elegant movements as they formed two lines, still whirling, and began to pass between each-other as though each line were a serpent weaving in and out of its fellow. Hands clapped and feet stamped in rhythm with the drums and the bells, drawing my attention, to the fact that the only parts of the dancers clearly on view were the hands beyond the wrists and the feet below the ankles. Even when the hands were raised to clap above shoulder-level, their veils stayed down. No matter how swiftly they whirled, the layers of vivid cloth covering them from crown to ankle never rose by more than a hand's breadth. Even when they gave elegant and dainty kicks, nothing above the ankle went on display. The effect was strangely enticing and I found it all too easy to see how this could be a dance dedicated to Eros, god of passion and procreation.

I was trying with all my strength to penetrate the veils and see whether Princess Deidamia was as lovely as her reputation suggested, when a kind of ripple went through the whole room. The dancers' steps faltered as the music died and the careful rhythm failed. I looked up and there was Queen Larisa, her face unveiled and anguished, standing at King Lycomedes' shoulder.

'My Lord,' she said. 'My Lord you must come. There is another… Another poisoning.'

***

All thoughts of the dance, the veils and the beautiful princess were driven out of my mind. At first I thought the still sickly

Prince Ajax had somehow been attacked again, such was the commotion that swept through the room. But it soon became obvious that this was something different. Whatever had occurred had happened in the women's quarters. This time the attempt had been more successful. Rhea, Princess Deidamia's nurse was all-but in the grip of Thanatos himself.

The poor woman's poisoning changed everything: it was far too near to King Lycomedes' beloved daughter for comfort. Within very few moments, therefore, the dancers had vanished and the women's quarters were declared open by the horrified king. Captain Adonis and his men were permitted to begin an immediate search. Which they started to do at once but with little immediate result, as it appeared they had no idea what they were actually looking for. Or who. Moreover, Adonis soon reported that identifying anyone except slaves, servants and the dying woman was well-nigh impossible. Although the rooms might be open, the veils stayed in place. It became clear that if Lycomedes wanted the investigation completed face to face, he would have to accompany the soldiers himself and order each veiled woman to expose her features for formal identification.

I was not surprised to find that the confused and frustrated Lycomedes turned to Odysseus in the end, begging him to take charge. It was Odysseus, after all, who had all-but saved Ajax. Perhaps he could perform the same magic on Rhea now that Hesira was among the dead. The queen intensified the urgency of the action needed when she emphasised how ill Rhea was: drooling, convulsing and unable to speak.

Odysseus could hardly refuse the anguished parents' request. Queen Larisa herself stood ready to guide him, veil still folded back and face set in grim determination. It seemed that Deidamia's father was not the only one worried about the sickly princess, who, much to my disappointment had not been well enough to lead the dance after all. Especially now that the one person she was happy to have tend her needed tending herself. Tending, and, if we weren't quick enough after all the fuss and hesitation, burying. Queen Larisa and her husband agreed with Odysseus' suggestion that Nestor should accompany him—for Nestor had known Medea and was assumed to have some expertise in the art of poisoning, therefore; especially as he boasted about it. And amid all the urgent bustle and confusion, no-one seemed to notice me when I followed the queen and the three kings into the forbidden corridors of Lycomedes' harem.

We did not go in through Lycomedes' secret entrance from which the queen had appeared to stop the dance with her terrible news, or along the passage I had already explored immediately behind it. Instead Queen Larisa led us through the palace and out onto the marble-flagged ledge where we had lost sight of the two veiled figures the night before. As we passed Ajax's chamber, Odysseus stepped into it. We waited outside while he spoke to the prince. When he emerged, he was holding a phial. 'This is what Hesira gave Ajax,' he said, showing it to the royal couple. 'He only swallowed half of it so there's plenty left. It was effective in his case. It might be effective in Rhea's.'

Queen Larisa nodded her agreement and then turned impatiently. As she strode on, I glanced back to see Ajax standing pensively watching us. His colour was partially restored and it looked as though his vigour was returning. Then I dismissed him from my mind as I turned to follow the queen. She led us out of the rear of the palace then across the ledge to a larger, more welcoming entrance. It seemed that the women's quarters were every bit as extensive and complicated as the general areas. They proved to be a maze of small rooms built along corridors that wove in and out of each other like the princesses in their serpentine dance. However, they all eventually led to a series of more substantial rooms then finally to a larger central area like Lycomedes' megaron. I was surprised at this complexity until I realised that the hierarchy of women in the harem might well demand it. Would the royal wives be happy to share accommodation with each-other? Possibly. With the lower concubines? Possibly not. With the princesses their daughters as they grew towards maturity? Conceivably—if the daughters were willing to share with their mothers, which the wilful Deidamia obviously was not. And none of them would be willing to share with the servants or the slaves. A glance into the megaron as we hurried past showed that Captain Adonis and his men were assembling all the women there. It was the structure of Princess Deidamia's quarters, however, that was most illuminating. Her personal chamber was approached along a short corridor. Immediately after the opening was a small room where her immediate handmaidens were housed. As we passed it, Queen Larisa gestured and the women in there followed us. After that came a slightly larger room where the unfortunate nurse lay gasping for breath, shuddering and drooling with a couple more women standing by her. They pulled down their veils as we entered. Further in again, glimpsed only as we went in to tend the poisoned nurse, was the princess's bedchamber itself, well furnished, well lit, with a comfortable-looking bed on which the princess was seated, her veil held in place by a slim silver headpiece from which little silver chains hung down.

Odysseus went straight to Rhea's head and gently lifted it. The queen herself stepped into her daughter's room, caught up a sizeable bowl which she found there, returned and held it ready. Odysseus pulled the drooling mouth open and poured the contents of Ajax's vial into it. Rhea choked a little. Her eyes flickered. She swallowed. As with Ajax, the result was immediate but fortunately the nurse had eaten and drunk little. What she puked up was easily contained within the bowl, which seemed particularly well-suited to the task. Within the inevitable stench of vomit there were strange odours of mice and honey. The mouse-smell I remembered from Ajax's poisoning and was obviously associated with hemlock poisoning, but I could not understand the honey to begin with.

Odysseus straightened. 'If Ajax is anything to go by, she will have a moment or two of lucidity no doubt brought on by the effort of vomiting. Then she will sleep; and wake in a few hours' time. If she is hungry when she does wake, perhaps she might have a little kykeon barley gruel without the goat's cheese.' He looked at the king, the queen and the serving women as Nestor nodded his agreement. 'It will be necessary to split the handmaidens' attention between Rhea and the Princess if you wish the nurse to recover.'

'Leave me, all of you,' came a quiet voice from Deidamia's chamber. 'I will do well enough on my own. Look after my poor

Rhea.'

iii

Deidamia had no sooner spoken that Rhea's eyelids fluttered. Queen Larisa bent over her, face to face, regal eyes blazing into the elderly, faded, flickering ones. 'Who did this?' she demanded.

'The queen,' came the faintest whisper. 'The queen sent honey cakes to Princess Deidamia but her stomach was too delicate… She gave them to me for she knows I love…'

There was no doubt in Lycomedes' mind which queen the whispering nurse was referring to. Rhea said more, but her words were lost beneath the orders the king was barking at the princess's handmaidens. By the time the poisoned nurse fallen back, fainting, Captain Adonis had been alerted to search out Queen Thetis and her women. Lycomedes and Larisa went to help the captain by insisting that veils be lifted on his command. Odysseus, Nestor and I were guided back to the megaron where we waited, like the crowd of Lycomedes' courtiers, listless in spite of the shock that these violent events had given us. But in fact the shocks were by no means over.

We had no sooner settled down than one of the guards I recognised from the first time I had entered the citadel's main gate came rushing in. 'Captain Adonis!' he gasped. 'Has anyone seen the captain? It's urgent!'

'He's in the women's quarters searching for Queen Thetis,' answered Odysseus. 'Is there anything we…'

'Queen Thetis!' interrupted the guard. 'But Queen Thetis is at the gate!'

'What do you mean?' snapped Nestor. 'What is she doing at the gate?'

'Lord Hypatios,' gabbled the guard. 'Lord Hypatios has summoned some men he had hidden in the city. They are holding the gate for the queen while she waits for her chariot!'

'Nestor!' snapped Odysseus. 'Take this man to King Lycomedes and Captain Adonis so he can report.' The old king's mouth opened but Odysseus continued relentlessly. 'It has to be you, old friend. No-one else would dare enter the women's quarters uninvited!'

Nestor saw the wisdom of Odysseus' words and obeyed at once. Odysseus swung round and ran out of the megaron with me as close behind him as I could manage. We were in the citadel's courtyard in moments, just in time to see Hypatios usher his black-robed, still-veiled queen up into the chariot. Her women were scrambling into the cart beside it. Odysseus and I pounded across the courtyard. 'Guards!' bellowed the captain. 'Guards close the gates!' But it was a forlorn hope. Not only did the order come far too late, the guards themselves were being held at sword-point by the men the drunken watch-keeper from *Nerites* had seen being hidden in the upper town in preparation for this very moment. Hypatios cracked his whip. The chariot rolled through the gates, gathering pace as it came onto the down-slope of the hill, then, in a cloud of dust, it was gone. The cart thundered out and down in its wake. The outsiders who had held the gate simply melted away so that by the time Odysseus and I reached it, there was nothing and no-one to be seen except the sheepish guards.

King Lycomedes appeared at the palace's main entrance with Nestor at one shoulder and Adonis at the other, his courtiers crowding behind him. 'What is it?' he called. Odysseus did not seem to hear the question, because he was deep in thought again, so I answered on his behalf. 'Queen Thetis and her women have gone, your majesty. Lord Hypatios has taken them all, no doubt to the ships waiting on the far side of the island.'

The king stopped in his tracks, his face a picture of conflicting emotions; the most obvious one was relief. I could see why. His murderous guest was gone. His harem, daughters, court and other guests were no longer under threat. If Odysseus was correct about Thetis' hold over him, then his secret was also safe. If his household was no longer at risk, then his life could return to its indulgent normality, with only Agamemnon's warlike demands to deal with. And after the last few days, those no doubt seemed like a relatively simple matter. It was as though great storm clouds had been hanging low over the citadel on the mountain peak, then a bright ray of sunshine had suddenly broken through them. 'A toast,' he said, clapping his hands. 'Come! Everybody back to the megaron! We must celebrate. There will be toasts.'

'Shall we not pursue them, Majesty?' asked Captain Adonis.

'Pursue them? Certainly not! We are well rid of them and that is the first toast I shall drink! To the megaron, everybody.'

***

'Perhaps,' suggested Odysseus, 'The young ladies could be persuaded to complete their dance. It is still early, there is much to celebrate as your majesty has observed, and in anticipation of the event that was so sadly interrupted I had ordered my men to visit my ship *Thalassa* and bring more gifts. These gifts are for the fair dancers themselves should you allow them to take them. We have all kinds of jewellery and adornments made of pearls and precious stones from beyond the empire of the Hittites and as far south as Egypt all set in silver and gold.'

The captain's voice rang all around the megaron, adding to the sense of festivity that had intensified with one toast after another until Lycomedes had called for his wives and daughters to join us. They all had, except for those tending Rhea, which included Princess Deidamia who was still consumed with guilt at the fact that honey-cakes meant for her had nearly killed the good old nurse instead. There was a rustle of excitement through the room at his suggestion. Lycomedes and Larisa exchanged glances, then capitulated in the face of their daughters' clear desire to complete their dance and see the presents brought to reward them for doing so.

The young women disappeared, no doubt to organise and prepare themselves. The atmosphere in the unusually crowded megaron was tense with expectation. Elpenor, Perimedes and Eurylocus appeared, all laden. As the musicians entered and settled themselves beside the fire pit, Odysseus helped his men arrange the gifts on the table in front of the king. They were precisely as he had described, together with polished silver mirrors. But then he turned on Elpenor with an uncharacteristic frown. 'You fool! Why did you bring these?' he demanded, lifting a pair of swords in jewel-encrusted scabbards with matching daggers. 'They were to remain aboard! Well, never mind.' He turned to the beaming king. 'When the dance is over, your majesty, and your lovely daughters have made their selection, please honour me by adding these to the gifts I have already given you.' He shook his head, glared at the unfortunate Elpenor and took his place once more.

The music started again. The young women whirled into the megaron in those two interweaving snakes, clapping and stamping as they span and danced. Even though I knew the beautiful princess Deidamia was not amongst them, I was still entranced; still sought to see beneath or through those veils to make out the faces of the beautiful young dancers. Alas, I had no success at all. They remained a dazzling whirl of colours. Red, yellow and blue in all shades, scarlet, crimson and indigo and even one costume in Tyrian purple, which I would have thought to have been Deidamia's had I not known where she was. The dancing grew faster and faster, the stamping and clapping louder and louder, the whirling so rapid that I felt as though my head was spinning rather than the dancers' lissom bodies. And then, just at the moment I believed the musicians could play no more quickly and the dancers could twirl no more wildly or interweave no more rapidly, it all stopped. Silence, so sudden and absolute that it seemed to echo. The dancers froze, then sank most gracefully into deep curtseys, their dresses and veils spreading in multicoloured pools upon the floor as though the lithe bodies were sinking like naiads beneath the surfaces of their gaudy little lakes.

There was a moment more of stillness. Lycomedes rose to lead the applause. As the megaron echoed to the storm of appreciation, the young women slowly straightened, seeming to rise out of their varicoloured pools. Even before the applause died, Lycomedes gave a broad gesture as though welcoming the princesses to his table—which in a way he was, but not to eat or drink. Shyly at first, they all moved towards the jewellery and trinkets, then, with increasing confidence, they began to go through the gleaming pile, spreading it along the table as they selected and tried on rings, bangles, necklaces and headpieces, swapping them amongst themselves as sisters often do, sharing rather than taking. How they could see to make their comparisons and their selections through the veils I shall never know. But so they did, until each princess, aided by her sisters, had selected what suited her best. They stepped back, curtsied to their father, curtsied to the generous guest who had supplied the precious finery and turned to go.

Ajax burst into the crowded megaron, blundering out of the corridor that led in from the courtyard. 'Attack!' he shouted. 'We're under attack!'

Odysseus automatically reached for the swords Elpenor had brought by apparent accident but they were gone. Two of the dancers, one in Spartan crimson and the other in Tyrian purple were standing, sword in hand, veils thrown back, narrow eyes searching for the enemy. 'Achilles,' said Odysseus softly, 'Patroclus. Welcome! We've been looking for you.'

'Odysseus!' shouted Ajax. 'this isn't part of your clever scheme. We really are under attack!'

We arrived in the circular courtyard in a shapeless crowd; the only ones amongst us properly armed were the young men dressed in women's garments. Odysseus scanned the place with a soldier's eye and when I followed his gaze I saw that there were men armed with bows and arrows in the four inward-looking towers and along the tops of the walls. Adonis and his guards stood disarmed and helpless once more, surrounded by yet more men. And in command of it all was Lord Hypatios.

'Not here, your majesty,' he called. 'If you ever want to see your pretty daughter Deidamia alive again you need to go to the ledge behind the palace. You'll find the princess waiting for you there with Queen Thetis keeping her company. Her majesty has one or two things she wants to discuss with you. And with you, Prince Achilles.'

iv

Unsurprisingly Lord Hypatios' words caused a good deal of confusion. The crowd of assorted guests, courtiers, servants and slaves—masculine and feminine—all turned at once, blocking the way so that what might have been a swift walk became slow and cluttered. Not even Ajax could force his way through. But the massive warrior made good use of the delay. 'I really don't understand all of this, Odysseus,' he rumbled. 'Just what in Hades' name is actually going on?'

'I suppose it had some of its origins in those six dead babies,' answered Odysseus. 'Did you know about Queen Thetis' babies? How they were all stillborn before Achilles arrived. They forged her as a smith takes copper and tin to forge into strong, sharp bronze. No wonder her love for the seventh son, the one that lived, also became something so dangerously sharp and strong. A love that wasn't tested, though, until Agamemnon called the boy to war and she realised she was going to lose him to death after all. But it also began in another place at another time. Not with the seventh birth but with the first murder.'

'When the apprentice rhapsode had his throat cut on the beach at Skopelos,' I said helpfully.

'No, lad,' said Odysseus. 'The first murder took place long before that and it took place here on Skyros. It's so obvious now I think about it – it's been in plain sight all along. The secret murder which gave Queen Thetis such a hold over Lycomedes when she somehow discovered the truth.' As he spoke we at last managed to force our way into the palace, but the corridors in front of us were still too crowded to allow swift passage. 'Imagine how it must have been all those years ago,' he continued. 'Young King Lycomedes, newly enthroned, not yet settled; with no firm grip as yet on his people the Dolopions. A youthful shadow of the man you see today. And what happens to him? The most popular and powerful hero still living resigns his kingship over Athens then arrives here on Skyros proposing to retire from public life and take up the position of a lowly farmer. The people flock to see him, to honour him; almost to worship him. The young king sees at once that his throne is all-but lost. That this would-be farmer, the ex-king Theseus of Athens, could take his kingdom away from him with no trouble at all. So what does he do? He befriends the old man. He offers to guide him round his farm, to show him the most advantageous places to plant his crops, his olive groves and his vines. The most verdant slopes to feed his flocks of sheep and goats. And then, at the pinnacle of the steepest and most precipitous of these slopes, he gives the old king a gentle push.

One push. As simple as that. Done in an instant with no looking back. And Theseus, what little they find of him at the bottom of the cliff, is no longer a threat.'

'Lycomedes murdered Theseus?' Ajax gasped. 'But that's monstrous! Unforgivable!'

'Indeed it is. And just imagine how Lycomedes' precious reputation would suffer if the facts were made public! At the time it would have ruined him. Even now, it would do some serious damage.'

'And Queen Thetis threatened to do just that?' demanded Ajax. 'Good thing too if she did it! Serve him right, the snake in the grass!'

'She threatened to do so unless Lycomedes did everything she demanded,' continued Odysseus as we approached the megaron along the passage from the courtyard. 'Starting with agreeing to offer Achilles and Patroclus a perfect hiding-place in his harem. They are light and swift—nothing like you, Ajax. Give them the dresses and the veils and they disappear amongst the women with no-one any the wiser. Which the king was happy to allow, because rumour, confirmed by Thetis no doubt, suggests that Achilles and Patroclus are more than friends. That they are, in fact lovers.'

'So that the women and girls in Lycomedes harem would be safe from their attentions,' I said.

'Precisely so,' he nodded. 'Everything settled down. Thetis and Peleus watched from a distance. Achilles was safely hidden. The Trojan campaign seemed far away. But then you arrived in Phthia, Ajax, and brought unpleasant reality with you. Agamemnon was clearly not going to forget about the smaller kingdoms like Phthia and Skyros and he was never going to take 'no' for an answer. He wanted Achilles and the Myrmidons and no alternative would do. Besides, you know Achilles better than anyone except Patroclus. You grew up together. You make no secret of the fact that Achilles would almost certainly leap at the chance to lead the Myrmidons into battle, were the offer to be made to him directly.'

'Peleus puts on the display designed to prove the Phthian army is the equal of the Myrmidons,' I said. 'But as you say, it's immediately obvious that there is no comparison between them.'

'And in fact Peleus has done himself more damage still,' added Odysseus. 'For both of us can now tell Agamemnon that Phthia should be able to supply an army of her own as well as Achilles' Myrmidons. Peleus panics. The instant you leave, he sends his rhapsode Dion to Scyros with a long, detailed message for Lycomedes. A message that is *so* long and complicated that only a rhapsode could commit it to memory but even so the old man has to share it with his apprentice.'

'And the message?' asked Ajax, forcing his way into the megaron at last, looking over the heads of everyone milling in there, then down at us beside him with a shrug and a shake of his head.

'That you must be deceived at all costs. That Lycomedes has to convince you that he has no idea where Achilles is and he simply must make you believe that, for the moment at least. However, in the longer term the two old kings must find a way to satisfy Agamemnon's demands or he will destroy them and their kingdoms. Therefore Lycomedes must begin to negotiate with the suddenly unwelcome guests in his harem how best to move the two young men back to Phthia and into command of the Myrmidons, ready for the Trojan campaign.'

'But what's to stop Achilles and Patroclus from just getting aboard the first ship and sailing home if I'm right and Achilles wants to go to war before all the glory goes to someone else?' asked Ajax.

***

'His mother, Queen Thetis,' answered Odysseus as we came level with the rhapsode's stool at the corner of the fire-pit. 'She announces that Achilles is almost certainly on Mount Pelion with his old tutor then pretends to sail north in search of him. Actually, she turns south and catches up with Dion's ship at Skopelos. She takes the chance of killing the apprentice there behind the screen of bushes designed to give her privacy and has two of her handmaidens get rid of the body. She moves from one ship to another and next morning as Dion's ship fights to pull free of a powerful west-flowing current and all hands are either at the oars or the sails, she stabs the rhapsode and pushes him overboard. In the confusion of changing course, no-one notices until it is too late to even think of attempting a rescue. She arrives at Skyros and sends word to Lycomedes. A well-armed contingent of her men is hidden in the city just outside the gates to the citadel. No-one notices except for one drunken watch-keeper on *Nerites*. She and her women are taken to the palace and vanish into the harem where she immediately seeks to control her son. But as she does so, she discovers to her horror that Lycomedes is not the only one with a deadly secret.'

'Who has a secret?' I asked as we passed the fire pit and pushed towards the opening of the passageway. 'And why is it so deadly?'

'The secret is simple and the young man tells it to his mother, as who would not?' said Odysseus. 'But it is not only Achilles' secret. It is Deidamia's and she dare not tell her parents. Indeed, she dare not tell anyone except her old nurse Rhea. She has lost her virginity to Achilles. Whether Patroclus and he are lovers or not, he finds the young princess irresistible. She has returned his passion, become his secret lover and is pregnant with his child.'

'And that changed everything?' Asked Ajax. 'How so?' He pushed out of the megaron into the constricted corridor. People turned to look at who was shoving them and when they saw who it was, they started giving way.

'I assume Deidamia warned Achilles and he passed the message on to his mother, that if King Lycomedes found out his beloved daughter was carrying Achilles' child then he would throw Achilles and Patroclus out without a second thought. The hold Thetis had over him, Theseus' murder, happened long ago and in the face of this immediate situation, the king would not hesitate. Suddenly Queen Thetis' motivation changed. In the short term at least, while she worked out how best to proceed, she had to stop anyone else discovering the truth about Deidamia's baby. Her task was complicated by Achilles himself. Being locked away was beginning to irritate him beyond measure. He needed someone of his own age to talk to; someone other than Patroclus and Deidamia. And someone suddenly appeared.'

'Me,' rumbled Ajax. 'But he never…' he slowed and looked back at us in confusion. We were about level with the door into his room; however he had all-but stopped moving.

'He never got the chance,' explained Odysseus, pushing the big man forward once again. 'Thetis would have found ways to stop him. Achilles would have known you were in the palace, though, and he would have been trying to have a word with you in secret no matter what his mother was up to. Thetis was torn with worry: had Achilles managed to see you without her knowing? What had he told you? Had he given away any secrets? Thetis could not be sure what you knew, so she took what she thought to be the safest way.'

'She poisoned me.'

'Precisely.'

'Then murdered Hesira the physician for saving me despite her?'

'It was more complicated than that,' said Odysseus. 'Deidamia was young and pregnant; too scared to tell anyone other than her nurse and her lover. Someone—probably Rhea herself—must have suggested that Hesira should be warned of the situation and then sworn to silence. But Hesira seemed untrustworthy to Thetis. He had too much freedom of movement. His first loyalties were to the princess' parents, not to the princess herself. He was simply too much of a risk. I believe it was not so much that he saved you, Ajax, but the fact that the confusion around your poisoning in the first place gave her an opportunity that was too good to miss. And so she took it.'

'But Rhea? Why harm the princess' only friend?' I wondered.

'I'm certain it was Rhea who advised warning the doctor. The situation must have seemed too dangerous to the old woman. She was not a midwife, remember, only a nurse. And she suddenly found herself in the presence of someone who had lost six babies one after the other. What if something similar should happen to her beloved princess? The pressure to warn someone else in the court must have been overwhelming. Thetis would have seen this, I'm, certain. And acted in the only way she had to hand.'

'The hemlock in the honey cakes?' I asked, glancing away up the passageway where we had first seen the two veiled figures trying to reach Ajax's room – who I realised must have been Achilles and Patroclus, disturbed in their mission to have a word with Ajax.

'The hemlock in the honey cakes' confirmed Odysseus.

'But why the cakes—why send them to the Princess. Was she also to be murdered?' I asked.

'No, lad. The one thing Queen Thetis knows more about than almost any queen is being pregnant; she's done it seven times after all. Pregnant women have desires that would seem strange were they not carrying a child. Things they must eat and things they cannot bear. I'm convinced she sent honey-cakes to the princess knowing full well even the smell of them would sicken her and she would pass them on to Rhea with her sweet tooth.'

'But the moment you unmasked Achilles and Patroclus everything changed again,' rumbled Ajax.

'Yes. I should have seen the outcome before I took the action. It was far more dangerous than I thought it would be. Thetis only pretended to run away. She never did. She now has another victim entirely in mind.

'Who?' asked Ajax as we pushed through at last onto the marble-flagged balcony behind Lycomedes' palace.

'Achilles himself,' answered Odysseus.

V

'Achilles?' I said, horrified. 'She's going to kill *Achilles*!'

'No, lad,' Odysseus gave a grim laugh. 'That would rather defeat her objective. She has been unable to stop the two old kings, even with her hold over the murderous Lycomedes. She has failed in her next objective of keeping Deidamia's pregnancy secret. Now she is threatening the one man who can stop everything she's so worried about with a single word.'

'And that is Achilles?' I asked, still unable to believe what he was saying. So surprised, indeed, that I did not register the vast emptiness that now surrounded us—perhaps also because we were still at the back of a crowd and not really able to see what was going on.

'Achilles himself,' nodded Odysseus, still forcing us forward in Ajax's wake. 'In this situation his strength is his weakness. Perhaps only a mother would see it and only someone as desperate as Thetis would use it. Achilles is motivated by honour. He is, indeed, the very personification of honour. If he swears to something, not even the gods themselves can make him break his word. So her plotting is all reduced to this one thing in the end. To make Achilles swear that he will never go to Troy.'

'But how will she do that if he's so keen to go?' I asked as we forced ourselves through the silent crowd, close behind Ajax, right to the very front. But then the huge warrior stepped aside and the answer to my question became obvious. Queen Thetis was standing on the very edge of the abyssal drop that lay beneath the end of the flagged ledge. She was turned almost sideways-on to the crowd, at whose centre, close to where we were standing, were King Lycomedes, Queen Larisa and Nestor, with the vivid figures of Patroclus and Achilles beside them. Queen Thetis was holding Princess Deidamia right on the lip of the precipice. A gentle tug would bring her back to safety. A gentle shove would send her over to her death.

'Momus, god of irony, must be laughing at this must he not, Lycomedes?' called Thetis across the stunned silence of the crowd as it stood watching her, horrified. 'That what established you so safely on your throne puts you in such a position now? The gentlest of pushes! Even gentler than the push you gave old Theseus, I would wager.'

'What do you want, Queen Thetis?' demanded Lycomedes, his voice trembling.

'Why, to talk to one of the lovely ladies of your harem, Your Majesty. To talk to my beautiful son!'

Achilles stepped forward, tall, slim and straight as a reed in his dress of Tyrian purple, his gold curls glinting as the wind ran through them and the sun struck them. 'I am here, Mother. What do you want?'

'*Your word*,' whispered Odysseus; and indeed, his lips moved in time with the speakers' through much of the following conversation as though he were the puppet-master and the other two were his puppets.

'Your word!' spat Queen Thetis.

'On what, Mother?'

'You know very well! Your word that you will never follow Agamemnon to Troy!'

'Consider, Mother,' said Achilles. 'If I give my word on this and abide by it as you know I will, then it is likely that my father will have to go in my place and the kingdom will be ruined.'

'Nonsense! You will rule in Peleus' place! Phthia will come to no harm by his absence. Besides, he will send General Argeiphontes with the army that so nearly bested your Myrmidons when Prince Ajax and the two kings were watching!'

'That has to have been a pretence, Mother. It can only be that my Myrmidons held back from destroying General Argeiphontes' men because the king my father requested it! Agamemnon will see through such a sham at once—assuming Ajax, Odysseus and Nestor have not done so already and do not tell him what they know! He will see through the pretence and have his revenge on Phthia. You should have no doubt about that.'

'Nevertheless,' shouted the desperate woman. 'If your father the king goes to Troy and dies beneath its walls or sends General Argeiphontes to do so and Phthia runs to ruin because of Agamemnon's anger, you will still be safe! Safe! That is all I desire!'

'I am a soldier, Mother! I was born to lead the Myrmidons. If I do not lead them to Troy, I will lead them to some other battlefield at some other time. It is my destiny and I cannot escape it by giving you my word. I cannot escape it, live or die.'

'Very well then!' Snarled Thetis. 'We will have the first casualty of this war you are so keen to join! Prepare to watch your pretty mistress die!' She tensed to push Deidamia over the edge.

'Just a moment, Your Majesty,' said Odysseus stepping forward. 'I have a suggestion to make, if you will do me the honour of listening to it.

***

'Well?' snarled Thetis, by no means pleased by this interruption.

'I would suggest, Majesty,' said Odysseus smoothly, 'that you are holding in your hands the solution to your problem.'

Queen Thetis looked at the terrified princess as though she was surprised to find her there. 'This child? How is she the answer to anything?'

'In herself, she is not, Majesty. But what lies within her might well be.'

'What on earth do you mean?' demanded Thetis.

'You are, quite understandably, fearful for the future of your son,' said Odysseus. 'These are dangerous days, full of calls to battle and preparations for war. Such things as tempt young men thirsty for glory and dangerous immortality. But the Princess there holds a surety for you. She bears your son's son. Your grandson who may be raised in peace and safety well away from these perilous times. A boy whose mother—or grandmother—might lavish all the love she may no longer be able to offer the boy's father. All it will take is a wedding.'

Thetis looked at the princess speculatively, though she did not yet pull her back from the edge. 'My son's son,' she said. 'And what if this whimpering creature has a daughter?'

'Then I would suggest that you might ask your son to give you his word on *that* matter. That if the princess is delivered of a daughter, then prince Achilles will return from whatever battlefield he is fighting in to remain by your side for as long as you wish. General Eudorus can lead the Myrmidons in his absence.'

Queen Thetis stood silently, her mind clearly racing.

'Majesty, it is a bargain you cannot possibly lose,' persisted Odysseus. 'Either you have the prospect of many joyful years of raising your son' son alongside the princess his mother, or you have the prospect of many joyful years with your son and his wife, raising your grand-daughter instead.'

'And would you give your word on that Achilles?' As Thetis turned to face her son and ask the question, she pulled the princess back from the edge of the precipice apparently without thinking.

'I would, Mother. I give my word that when the princess is delivered of our child, wherever I am and in whatever I am engaged, be it battle or preparation for battle, be it in Achaea or Asia, be it Troy or any of the cities of the Troad or the Trojan islands, I will return if the child is a girl and remain at your side and Deidamia's while we raise her as a princess of Phthia. But if my wife is delivered of a son, then you and my father together with my wife may have the raising of him.'

'In Phthia!' snapped Lycomedes. 'Why in Phthia?'

'It is traditional for the bride to go to the husband's house, Majesty,' said Achilles. 'Besides, how could I want my daughter or my son to be raised at the court of the murderer who pushed the great King Theseus off a cliff?'

'I am satisfied,' announced Thetis. She pulled Deidamia right away from the edge and pushed her towards Achilles. 'You may take your princess and have your wedding. Take your Myrmidons and go your way. But she comes to me in Phthia before she comes to term!'

Even Ajax had had trouble pushing through the crowd to get us here from the gates but the throng seemed simply to melt before Queen Thetis as she strode through the palace to the circular courtyard that fronted it. Achilles and Deidamia, Lycomedes and Larisa, Ajax, Nestor, Odysseus and I followed closely behind them. By the time we came out of the great entrance, Thetis had crossed the courtyard and mounted her chariot—his time for real. She turned away from us, grasped the front, and never looked back as Hypatios drove her out through the gates.

I looked across the crowd as the chariot vanished down the hill. Beside us at the front of the palace, Achilles was standing with Deidamia's head on his shoulder. His left arm was clasped gently round her waist. In his right fist he still held the sword he snatched up in the moment Odysseus' trap revealed his true identity. Patroclus stood beside him, also embracing one of the princesses, this one wearing an indigo veil; he was also clutching the sword which had given him away. King Lycomedes and Queen Larisa stood side by side as though stunned and Captain Adonis worked at mustering and re-arming his men now that the invaders had gone with their queen. I looked at Odysseus. 'And so she has won,' I said. 'All those murders, achieved and attempted, all to ensure that one thing which she now has won! Her heart's desire, and not a whiff of punishment! It makes you doubt the Fates! The gods themselves! How could such evil win such happiness?'

'I don't think you quite understand, lad,' said Odysseus. 'What has all the stabbing, slitting and poisoning actually won for her in the end? Somebody else's baby. It will never be her own; flesh of her flesh. I have no doubt Deidamia will be delivered of a son—how could it be otherwise? But she will never dote on him as she doted on her Achilles. And even if he turns out to be Achilles reborn, she must share him with his mother if not with his father. And if he *is* Achilles reborn, then she will simply have to go through this terrible heartache all over again in twenty years or so, for there will always be wars and a son like Achilles' son will always be hungry for glory.

'And in the meantime, what has she really won? She will still have the terror she will feel with every report from whatever battlefield her golden boy is fighting on. She will still dream every night that he is dying or dead. Still look for his death in every augury and oracle. Still waste her life praying to gods, who are all too deaf, that they should protect him, keep him safe from terrible Thanatos. And she will do all this in the sure and certain knowledge that one day her nightmares will come true. One day the report will come. In the mud and the blood of some far field Achilles will have fallen. And her seventh son will have joined his six brothers and all of them at last are dead.'

SOURCES

Major source:
The Iliad new Penguin edition tr Martin Hammond
Also tr Caroline Alexander
Also tr E V Rieu
Also tr George Chapman
The Odyssey tr E V Rieu

Online etc:
Michael Wood *In Search of The Trojan War* (BBC)
Ancient History Documentary *The True Story of Troy* An Ancient War.
The Trojan War & Homeric Warfare
The Trojan War - Myth or Fact
The Truth about TROY
Great Battles: Was there a Trojan War? Recent Excavations at Troy
Naue II: Mycenaean Bronze Sword Tests
The Trojan War Episode 2: Weapons and Armour During The Trojan War

Academic sources:
The Book of Swords Richard Francis Burton
Mediterranean Portrait of a Sea. Ernle Bradford
Greek Mythology – The complete guide
Bulfinch's *Mythology* Thomas Bulfinch
The War That Killed Achilles Caroline Alexander
The Wooden Horse – The liberation of the Western mind from Odysseus to Socrates Keld Zeruneith *The Wooden Horse* - Some Possible Bronze Age Origins - I. Singer (ed), Luwian and Hittite Studies.

Creative sources:
The Silence of the Girls Pat Barker
The Song of Troy Colleen McCullough
The Song of Achilles Madeline Miller
Troy Adele Geras
NB All 'Songs' are based on Ancient Greek poems adapted from various translations.

Made in the USA
Las Vegas, NV
19 July 2021

26662283R00100